1775

... Then the bagpipes' wail
pierced the soft October evening,
silencing even the tree frogs in the deep forest
beyond the clearing. Elspeth felt a familiar, unwelcome
shiver skitter down her backbone. *Céilidhs* were fun
celebrations, times for Scottish people to gather
for storytelling and music and dancing. But she
never heard bagpipes without thinking of
the stories she'd been raised on, tales of
pipers leading Highland men
into bloody battle. . . .

ELSPETH'S WORLD
North Carolina in 1775

Aunt Mary's home

Sweetwater Creek

Elspeth's home

The Blairs' home

MacRackens' mill

Panther Creek

Black Bull Tavern
in Cross Creek

Village of
Cross Creek

Wilmington Road

BETRAYAL AT CROSS CREEK

❧

by
Kathleen Ernst

American Girl®

Visit our Web site at **americangirl.com**

Printed in the United States of America.
04 05 06 07 08 09 RRD 10 9 8 7 6 5 4 3 2 1

History Mysteries® and American Girl®
are registered trademarks of Pleasant Company.

PERMISSIONS & PICTURE CREDITS
The following individuals and organizations have generously given permission
to reprint illustrations contained in "A Peek into the Past": p. 155—photo of
piper, Digital Vision/Getty Images (DV0301982); pp. 156–157—Highlands photo,
© www.danheller.com; cabin, courtesy of North Carolina Office of Archives and
History; longleaf pines © David Muench/Corbis; woman at loom, John Dominis/Getty
Images; overshot samples and pattern drafts, Collection of the Museum of Early Southern
Decorative Arts, Winston-Salem, NC; pp. 158–159—hanged effigy, North Wind Picture
Archives; *Bostonians Paying the Exciseman* by Philip Dawe, The John Carter Brown Library at
Brown University; Highland soldier, illustrated by Angus McBride/© Osprey Publishing Ltd.;
pp. 160–161—portrait of Flora MacDonald by Allan Ramsay; battle scene, National Park
Service, Harpers Ferry Center Commissioned Art Collection, artist, Gilbert Cohen;
Loyalists leaving for Canada, etching by Howard Pyle for *Harper's Weekly*;
dancers, image © 1998 by Jay J. Pulli, pulli@elohi.com.

Cover and Map Illustrations: Jean-Paul Tibbles
Line Art: Greg Dearth

**Library of Congress Cataloging-in-Publication Data
available on request.**

With thanks to:

My parents, for raising me on books;

And Peg Ross, for being so Midwestern

TABLE OF CONTENTS

CHAPTER I
BETRAYED

The Gunns' party was already in fine swing when Alasdair MacKay brought out his great bagpipes. Elspeth shot a sidelong look at Mercy Blair, her best friend. Mercy seemed to be enjoying the gathering. But unlike Elspeth and the other guests, Mercy was not Scottish. She'd been born here in North Carolina Colony to English-born parents. When the Gunns had invited their friends and neighbors to a *céilidh* celebrating the end of harvest, and Grannie suggested inviting Mercy, Elspeth had fretted for a week before making up her mind. Now that Mercy was here, Elspeth *so* wanted her to enjoy herself!

The party had spilled from the Gunns' cabin into the clearing as the sun dipped behind the trees. Some of the guests shouted encouragement as Alasdair slung the bagpipes in place. "Go on wi' ye, laddie! Play us a reel!"

"What are they saying?" Mercy whispered.

Elspeth thought through her words, for she knew that other colonists had trouble understanding the Scottish immigrants even when they *did* speak English. "Most everyone is speaking Gaelic, as we did back in Scotland. And some of it is Scots English. That's Alasdair MacKay. He's the best piper in the settlement. Everyone is . . . what's the word? Cheering? Yes, they're cheering him on."

Some of the men wore breeches with their loose linen shirts, but Alasdair wore a tartan belted plaid from the Scottish Highlands—a long length of wool gathered around his waist and slung over one shoulder. He grinned, flexing his fingers. Then the bagpipes' wail pierced the soft October evening, silencing even the tree frogs in the deep forest beyond the clearing.

Elspeth felt a familiar, unwelcome shiver skitter down her backbone. *Céilidhs* were fun celebrations, times for Scottish people to gather for storytelling and music and dancing. But she never heard bagpipes without thinking of the stories she'd been raised on, tales of pipers leading Highland men into bloody battle.

Mercy stared at Alasdair with wide-eyed astonishment, but a smile slowly shaped her mouth. And when Alasdair stopped to empty a tankard of ale and one of the MacFarlane boys reached for his fiddle, Mercy turned to Elspeth with delight. "I've surely never heard such music!" she whispered. "Oh, thank you for bringing me!"

Elspeth felt the knot of worry in her chest ease. Her Scottish neighbors, who usually kept tight with their own, had welcomed Mercy into their circle. Now, if they could just get through the evening without trouble! Scots rarely gathered together without someone railing against the troubles in Scotland that had sent waves of emigrants over the ocean to America.

Lately, adults often ranted about troubles right here, too. Elspeth knew that they worried about the political arguments flaring throughout the colonies. Some of the American colonists were angry with King George and the British government about unfair taxes. Men called Patriots wanted revolution against the British king—why, there had already been fighting at places called Lexington and Concord in the northern colony of Massachusetts. Here in North Carolina, Patriots had forced the royal governor to flee. But many people throughout the colonies did not want revolution. They were known as Loyalists. They were willing to fight, too.

And in North Carolina, both of these groups wanted the Scottish immigrants to join their cause.

Just this one evening, Elspeth thought hopefully. *Let us have just one evening without anger and bitterness.* Her chest eased a bit more as she saw that tonight, people seemed more interested in enjoying themselves than in arguing. Children darted across the clearing. The older girls and boys began to dance—lively jigs and reels and the whirling circular dance called "America." Elspeth's cousins, Robbie and Duncan MacKinnon, had no trouble finding girls to dance with. The boys also wore plaids for the occasion and looked, Elspeth thought, quite fine.

Her chest tightened as her grandfather's booming voice cut through the music—but Grandda was telling jokes, no more. *Don't fret so much!* she scolded herself. Even Grannie seemed to be enjoying herself. Grannie and Aunt Mary were helping the other women spread baskets of hoecakes and scones, dishes of turnips and sweet potatoes and beans, and platters of turkey and venison on tables set up near the cabin.

Elspeth nudged her friend. "Let's get something to eat."

Elspeth and Mercy joined the line behind a girl about their age. She had corn-colored hair and a face speckled as a meadow pipit's egg. *"Ciamar a tha thu?"* the girl asked shyly.

"I am well," Elspeth answered. "But do ye speak English? My friend Mercy here doesna have Gaelic. I'm Elspeth Monro. Are ye newly arrived?" The other girl looked confused, so Elspeth repeated herself in Gaelic.

"My name's Jennet MacRacken. I *am* just arrived." Jennet's words tumbled over each other in her eagerness. "My father—he's called Tall Tam MacRacken—decided that we'd come to America and start fresh. It's just us two—my mother died years ago. We're staying with my father's brother. He owns the mill on Panther Creek."

Elspeth felt a kinship to any girl who'd lost her mother, just as she had. Still, she felt awkward chattering in Gaelic in front of Mercy and was glad when Grannie beckoned. "We're sure to meet again," she told Jennet.

"I hope so." Jennet's smile included both girls.

Elspeth and Mercy joined Grannie as she pulled a dish from beneath a linen towel. "My crowdie's almost gone," she told Elspeth in Gaelic, waving flies away. Unlike Grandda, Grannie didn't speak English. "I saved a bite for Mercy."

"Thank you." Elspeth smiled. Grannie was not a prideful woman, except where her cooking was concerned. Her crowdie, made from oatmeal and whipped cream and a bit of brown sugar, *was* good.

Grannie leaned close. "Stay clear of that MacRacken girl," she muttered to Elspeth. "There's bad blood there."

Elspeth's smile faded. "Grannie—" she began, but the old woman had turned aside. Fortunately, Jennet was already walking away. The man who joined her, long and lean as a hoe handle, must be her father.

"Elspeth, what are these?" Mercy pointed.

"Bannocks? They're oatcakes. Baked on a griddle. I hardly ever get them here, but we ate them back home."

Mercy eyed the bannocks dubiously. "How is it that you speak English, when most Scottish people don't?"

"My grandda learned when he was a soldier, years ago."

Elspeth scooped a dollop of mashed turnips onto her plate. "And he taught me. Here, try one of my Aunt Mary's sausages."

Elspeth and Mercy sat on a log to eat and watch the dancing. As twilight's purple shadows faded into the rich black of full night, some of the boys built a bonfire. Elspeth stared at the sparks shooting skyward. *We could be back in Scotland,* she thought. Two years had passed since she and her mother's parents, Angus and Morag MacKinnon, had arrived in North Carolina. Still, moments like this took her back: the bagpipes, the Gaelic songs, the bonfire, the mesmerizing swirl of men's plaids and ladies' skirts as the dancers whirled . . .

But no—the night smelled of pine, not of heather and the sea. The Gunns' log home was more substantial than the smoke-blackened sod-and-stone cottages the Highlanders had inhabited in Scotland. And her best friend was an American!

Many of the youngest guests were sleeping on laps and shoulders when Grannie came for the girls. "It's time we were heading home," she said to Elspeth. "Did your friend enjoy herself?"

When Elspeth translated, Mercy beamed. "Oh, yes, Mistress MacKinnon, I had a lovely time!" Grannie nodded at Mercy's enthusiasm, and a small smile touched her own lips. Night cloaked the shiny red scars of a long-ago fire that marred her face.

Soon Grannie, Grandda, Elspeth, and Mercy stood in a little cluster of people saying their good-byes. Beyond them, near the fire, the musicians were still at it. Elspeth tapped her fingers longingly against her leg in time to the rollicking tune.

"Elspeth Monro, you've fetched on an inch since I saw you last," a neighbor said with a smile.

"It was fine to meet ye, Mercy," a young woman called.

"Send Elspeth over soon to help me pick wild grapes, if you can spare her," Aunt Mary told Grannie.

"Grandda," Robbie said, "some of the lads want your opinion of the Patriots' latest handbill." He held out a crumpled piece of paper. Elspeth saw a pine tree and a snake pictured below the printed words. "Can Duncan and I bring the boys by your place, once I round them up?" He gestured toward the stomping and twirling black shadows silhouetted against the bonfire.

Elspeth frowned. These handbills held political arguments and often were nailed up or passed out in the nearby village of Cross Creek. Patriots' rebellious ideas angered the Loyalists, who responded by printing their own ideas. Jings! Just what she did *not* want to hear about tonight!

But Grandda shook his head. "I'll no' be home for a bit. I'll leave off your grannie, then take Elspeth's friend on to home. She lives by Cross Creek."

Robbie looked disappointed but nodded. "Another

time, then. If your wheat's ready, Grandda, we'll come this week and help thresh." Robbie and Duncan and Grandda often worked together to get chores done on the two little farms, which were only a mile or so apart.

Grandda had brought their market cart and Moll, their gray mare. Grannie and Grandda sat on the seat, and Elspeth and Mercy settled in the back. "Did ye truly have a fair time?" Elspeth whispered as they headed into the night.

"Yes! Why do you keep asking?"

"Oh . . . your mother and father have been so kindly to me. I do love coming to your house." Elspeth felt her face grow hot. "I've felt more than a wee bit ashamed of no' returning the kindness."

"Well, you're not entirely a guest at our house," Mercy pointed out. "You're practically an apprentice. My mother says she could never keep up with her orders if she didn't have your help at the looms."

"Still." Elspeth's grandmother and Mercy's mother had worked out a trade: Mistress Blair was teaching Elspeth to weave, and the MacKinnons kept the Blairs supplied with sweet potatoes and kale and such. The Blairs often invited Elspeth to stay for supper, and she had dithered for months about inviting her friend to dinner in return. If only Grandda didn't so often shout. If only Grannie didn't so often disappear, cold and quiet, into her memories of an old Scottish civil war . . .

Mercy squeezed Elspeth's hand. "Never mind,"
she said. "As for tonight, it was fun! What did you call
the party?"

"A *céilidh*."

"Kay-lee." Mercy tried the Gaelic word. "I loved
the music, and the dances, and the food—well, excepting
perhaps the oatcakes," she added fairly, and Elspeth
laughed.

They stopped first at the MacKinnons' cabin on the
banks of Sweetwater Creek. Elspeth carried their food
baskets inside. Grannie lit two candles and placed one
in the window. "Tell Mercy I want to send the rest of
this venison home with her," she told Elspeth. "Wait
while I fetch a smaller basket."

The basket in hand, Elspeth and Mercy curled together
again in the cart. "We won't be gone overlong," Grandda
called to Grannie. "Come on, Moll. Up with ye now."

The trail Grandda followed was barely wide enough
for the cart. The quarter moon couldn't reach through
the thick trees, and the punched-tin lantern on the seat
beside Grandda cast only flecks of feeble light. In the
Scottish Highlands, Elspeth had lived on the Isle of Skye,
a place of craggy green and gray hills, and moorlands of
low-growing heather. She didn't like North Carolina's
deep forests of pine, oak, sycamore, and magnolia. The
towering trees, sometimes overhung with moss and
mistletoe, made Elspeth feel nervy—especially at night.

She was glad when Grandda began to sing an old Scottish ballad. The familiar song almost lulled her to sleep—but suddenly he stopped mid-phrase and pulled Moll to a halt. Elspeth jerked upright. "Grandda—"

"Wheesht!" he whispered, and jerked a hand in her direction: *be still.* Mercy sat up silently beside her. Then Elspeth heard what had caught Grandda's attention: a saddle's creak, slow hoofbeats. Coming toward them. Who would ride without a lantern on such a dark night?

"Take the lines, *Elisaid,*" Grandda whispered. Elspeth reached over the cart's seat and felt the heavy leather lines pressed into her suddenly shaking fingers.

The rider approached them. No—riders. Three, four? Elspeth wished she could scrape away the darkness. One of the horses crashed into the forest litter to the right of the cart—and another to the left. Her heart began to skitter in her chest. Mercy clutched her arm like a carpenter's vise.

"Angus MacKinnon!" The rider in front of the cart was a faint shadow. His voice was rough, low—and definitely not Scottish.

"And who might ye be?"

"A Patriot."

"I'll be wondering why ye and your friends see fit to stop me on a dark night." Grandda's voice was even, but tight.

"To give warning. We understand that the former

royal governor of North Carolina is plotting with Scots
to regain control of the colony."

"And why're ye telling this to me?" Grandda rose
slowly to his feet. He was not an overly tall man, but he
was strong and solid-built as an oak. Elspeth saw his flint-
lock pistol in his right hand. His left hand gripped the
small knife he always carried in his stocking. He held both
weapons pressed against his plaid but at the ready. Elspeth's
mouth went dry.

"To make sure you understand that the Patriots of
this colony will not permit the former governor to return.
You are known and respected by many Scots in this settlement and can influence the younger men. You would be
wise to—"

"Are ye tellin' me my business?" Grandda demanded.
"By God! I'll no' have any man tell me my business." His
fingers flexed on the handle of his knife. Elspeth's palms
were so slick with sweat, it was hard to grip the lines.

The speaker shrugged. He seemed to be wearing a
tricorn hat, pulled low over his forehead. "It's everyone's
business. And we need to know this: are you Patriot or
Loyalist?"

Grandda bent his knees slightly, as if tensing for a
spring. "I'll no' be tellin' you!"

"We Patriots are prepared to fight and die for our cause.
And we're prepared to strike against those who don't—"

"And now ye dare to threaten me?" Grandda roared.

"Do ye think I'm some skulkin' wee lad to be sent running home with my tail 'tween my legs? *Beul sìos oirbh!* You're an ill-raised devil to provoke a man whilst he's ferryin' two wee lassies. But if it's a stramash you're wanting, by God I'll give ye more than ye bargained for! I fought at Culloden, ye numpty gowks!"

A horse whickered behind them. Elspeth bit her tongue. They were surrounded. Her hands cramped on the reins. Mercy's fingers bit into her arm.

"Angus MacKinnon, you have been warned," the lead rider said finally. "Come along, boys."

Elspeth heard sticks snap as the three riders in the woods joined the fourth waiting behind them on the trail. They melted into the black night as Angus MacKinnon bellowed a few final curses and insults after them in a scorching jumble of Gaelic and English.

Elspeth closed her eyes, willing her heart to ease back to normal. The reins slipped from her numb fingers, but Moll, bless her placid hide, didn't move. Mercy slowly eased her grip on Elspeth's arm.

"They're gone," Grandda said finally. "Are ye both all well?"

"I—I think so," Elspeth stammered. "Who were they?"

"Naught but trouble. We'll get Mercy on to home now." He picked up the lines and called to Moll. The wooden wheels creaked as the cart lurched forward, and Elspeth sank back down beside her friend.

"Sweet heavens!" Mercy whispered. "I didn't know what to think."

"'Tis sorry I am for all that," Elspeth whispered back. She wanted to cry. The night was ruined!

"It's not your fault. I was frightened for a moment, but no harm came of it." Mercy leaned closer. "What did your grandfather say to them? I couldn't understand half of it."

Elspeth tried to remember. "He said that if they wanted a fight, he'd give them more than they bargained for . . . and called them stupid fools. The other Gaelic bits . . . well, it wasn't polite."

When they reached Mercy's home, Mistress Blair guided her husband, who was nearly blind, out to meet them with lantern in hand. Elspeth chewed her lip as Grandda explained what had happened. Would the Blairs say Mercy couldn't visit Elspeth again?

But once assuring themselves that Mercy was well, Mr. Blair only thanked Grandda for seeing her safely home. "These are troubled times," he said grimly. "We'd best be keeping indoors after dark. Do you wish to stay the night?"

"Nae. I thank ye, but Morag's waiting on to home," Grandda said. "Those cowards said their piece, and they heard mine. I dinna expect any more trouble tonight."

Mercy hugged Elspeth good-bye. "Thank you again. I'll look for you tomorrow. And don't worry!"

Don't worry—that's easy for Mercy to say, Elspeth thought as she and Grandda headed back into the brooding forest. Mercy hadn't been raised in Scotland. Mercy didn't know what real trouble was.

Grandda put his arm around Elspeth's shoulders. "Ye did fine back there, lass. Just fine. Your grannie'd be proud." He usually spoke English when they were alone.

Elspeth stared at the bits of lantern light cast upon her shoes. Grandda hadn't known how scared she'd been. Grannie was a woman of great courage. Elspeth's own mother wouldn't have been frightened either. Both had stood up to far worse during the Scottish troubles thirty years earlier, when Elspeth's mother was only ten—two years younger than Elspeth was now! If Grannie had seen Elspeth's hands trembling, she most certainly would not have been proud.

Elspeth sighed. A storm of trouble was brewing on the horizon—she felt it down to her bones. "The question that man asked, about whether ye favor Patriots or Loyalists. Which is it to be?"

Grandda paused. "My mind is no' yet decided."

Elspeth stared at the darkness as they rumbled along the narrow forest track, gritting her teeth when something rustled off to her right. What might be waiting ahead— more Patriots? Maybe a band of Loyalists this time? Or perhaps just a wee bear or bobcat? She gripped the seat tightly, wanting nothing more than to be back home.

Then she glanced at her grandfather, ramrod-straight and vigilant, and felt some better. "Grandda," she said, "these troubles don't have to bother us, aye? Such men are likely to hide in darkness, and it's a rare night we roam about. We can just stay out of it."

Grandda shook his head. "I'm no' so sure of that, Elspeth. What happened tonight was nae coincidence."

His tone made Elspeth's mouth go dry all over again. "What do ye mean?"

"Those scoundrels knew who I was without askin'. They called me by name. They knew we were about tonight—and that we'd no' be taking our usual path home." Grandda's voice quivered with anger. "Elspeth, lass, we were betrayed."

Elspeth lay in bed staring into the shadows. *Betrayed.* Only their Scottish friends at the *céilidh* had known Angus MacKinnon's route that night. Had one of them gotten word to the Patriots, hoping to force Grandda to declare himself? Who would have done such a thing?

And...why? Despite what the Patriot had said, Elspeth knew that the Scottish men of *real* influence were the wealthy merchants and those who had arrived with money enough to purchase plantations along the Cape Fear River valley's fertile bottomlands. Grandda paid rent for his scrap of piney woods, and for ten more years would owe half of his crops to the rich man who'd paid for their passage to the colony. His opinion ruled Robbie and Duncan, of course, and it might sway some of the other threadbare Scots struggling to make a new start in this new land. Was that enough to warrant the Patriots' cocked pistols and threats?

Elspeth could not sleep for worrying. Besides, Grandda was still stomping about below, reliving in Gaelic the encounter with the Patriots for his wife. "And mark me, the troubles are only going to get worse," Grandda declared. "I don't like the way the wind is blowing. You should keep Elspeth close to home until this business is seen through."

Elspeth caught her breath and sat up in bed.

"I'll not have Elspeth lose her chance to learn a trade just because some drunken hotheads ride about at night," Grannie protested.

Grandda's voice rose. "You'd risk bringing your grand-daughter to harm—"

"And what do you know of risk or harm for a girl, Angus MacKinnon? The greatest risk comes from raising a girl-child with no means to support herself. A skilled woman may not have to hear her children whimper as they starve. I'll not have Elspeth as ill-prepared for the world as I was when you went off—"

"And you're thinking that when I joined the prince's army in '45 I was off on a lark, are you? By God, woman, you have no notion of what we lived through..."

Elspeth burrowed under the coverlet, pushed her fingers into her ears, and tried to sleep.

By the time Elspeth came down the ladder from the loft next morning, Grandda had already gone. Grannie stood before the huge fireplace in the main room, stirring oatmeal porridge bubbling in an iron kettle hung over the fire. In the early morning light, the scars on the old woman's face showed pink and angry.

Elspeth hesitated, rubbing her arms. Sometimes arguments with Grandda left Grannie pricklish for days. Worse, sometimes Grannie had confused spells after talking about that long-ago war in Scotland, as if she was living those terrible days again.

"Fetch this off, will you, child?" Grannie pointed at the heavy kettle with the wooden spoon she held in her left hand.

Relieved, Elspeth hurried to do her bidding. Grannie's right hand hung useless—another legacy of the war in Scotland. *Be patient,* Elspeth reminded herself. If Grannie was stubborn and cross, she had good cause.

As the two sat down at the puncheon table for breakfast, Elspeth choked down a powerful wave of loneliness. It was *hard* sometimes, being the only one left with Grannie and Grandda. Elspeth had never known her mother, who'd died two hours after Elspeth was born. But she remembered her father, who'd died of sickness when Elspeth was five. And she sorely missed her three older sisters, all married and living in Scotland with their own families.

Grannie broke the silence. "I need your help cleaning

this morning, and I've a mind to render down the last of the lard. But I want you to run along to Mistress Blair's after."

Elspeth nodded, trying to keep her relief from showing.

"Your grandfather thinks it's best if you take the hunting path around, instead of the main trail," Grannie added calmly. "Do you know the way?"

"Yes," Elspeth said. Using the network of hunting paths would make the trip through the woods even longer, but she'd stand up to that gladly if it meant she could still visit Mercy.

When Grannie went to feed the chickens, Elspeth washed the dishes. She scrubbed the cabin's fine floor (made of mill-sawn boards!) with sand, then found a clean dusting rag. When they immigrated, the family had brought only one trunk, filled with clothes and a few treasured mementos. The bed in the corner, the pine cupboard, the table, the iron kettles, the storage barrels and pewter dishes—all had been acquired since the MacKinnons' arrival. After only two years in North Carolina, the family was already better off than they'd been in Scotland. Their success had come from back-breaking work, and the colony's sweltering summer heat and clouds of mosquitoes were hard to bear. Still, Elspeth never went to bed hungry.

Now more *trouble* threatened! Elspeth felt as if a dark storm cloud had followed the Scots all the way across the Atlantic Ocean. "Grannie," she dared when the old woman came back inside, "do you think those Patriot men will cause more harm if Grandda doesn't declare himself for their cause?"

"I think men were born on earth to cause harm," Grannie said. "You should learn that well. Your mother learned it soon enough."

Elspeth paused, her dust rag poised above an earthenware bottle with a lovely calico pattern. Elspeth's mother, Peggy, once had saved this very bottle when British soldiers set fire to the MacKinnon home. Elspeth often imagined the soldiers' shouts, the sudden hiss and crackle of flames on the thatched roof, the smell of smoke. Young Peggy'd had the presence of mind to snatch up her baby brother, a sack of oats, *and* the bottle before fleeing. "Without it, we'd have had nothing to hold water during the weeks we spent hiding in the heather," Grannie had said.

Could I ever be so brave? Elspeth wondered, dusting the precious bottle reverently. She couldn't imagine it. With a sorry sigh, she eased the bottle back to its place of honor on the mantel—right below Grandda's old broadsword, which hung on the wall.

When the cabin was tidy, Elspeth built a fire under the big kettle in the yard. From a bin in the barn, she began hauling chunks of fat from their last hog butchering. As she and Grannie began to melt the fat, another worry popped into her mind. "Grannie, why don't you want me to talk to Jennet MacRacken? She—"

"Wheesht!" Grannie whirled upon Elspeth with a fierce look. "Do not *ever* speak that name to me!"

Elspeth stared at her. *Mo chreach!* she thought. *Good heavens!* Whatever had some member of the MacRacken clan done to make Grannie so angry?

They rendered the fat and strained it clean in silence. By then, Elspeth was streaked with grease and overtired of the stench of lard. Her grandfather was visible through the trees, digging the last of their sweet potatoes. He'd be ready for a meal soon enough, and Elspeth wasn't eager to sit down with *both* of her grandparents. It took more than a day for their arguments to blow away. And her own question about the MacRackens had further soured Grannie's mood.

"The lard'll keep 'til you're ready to make soap," she told her grandmother. "I'll hang that barley broth over the fire, then be away to the Blairs'. Unless you need something else?"

But Grannie shook her head. "Go on with you."

With a basket of fresh-picked kale over her arm, Elspeth hurried along the hunting trails that wound toward Cross Creek. Such gloomy, flat, endless forest! Even when the oaks and elms and sycamores shed their leaves for winter, the longleaf pines would still shadow the woods. *Pine*—the tree that provided wood and pitch and turpentine and tar. Elspeth knew much of North Carolina's trade depended on pine trees. And she knew that British trade laws, which ensured that the British profited from the colonists' labor, were among those that made the colonists most angry.

Elspeth's nerves crackled. What if she encountered one of the Patriots who had threatened Grandda? Surely Patriots wouldn't strike during daylight. And surely they wouldn't bother a wee girl . . . would they? Elspeth wished she hadn't heard her grandfather last night: *You'd risk bringing your granddaughter to harm?* His words followed her like a stalking panther all the way to the Blairs' house.

Her friends lived in a clapboard house on the outskirts of Cross Creek, a busy trading village located on a hill above a branch of the Cape Fear River. Every day, back-country farmers rumbled into town in wagons heavy with produce to sell or trade, or with grain to be ground at one of the gristmills. Men working the pine trade hauled lumber and tar to storehouses by the river before rafting the goods downstream to Wilmington. Merchants filled their shelves with needles, buckets, nutmegs, hinges—anything farm families couldn't produce themselves.

Mercy was plucking a butchered chicken in her yard. "Elspeth!" she cried happily, dropping the bird on her bench. She tried without much success to wipe pinfeathers from her hands. "Mother's out fetching some wool, but she'll be so pleased to see you."

"And I'm surely pleased to be here," Elspeth confessed. "Everything's in a stramash at home." She sat down and told Mercy about Grandda and Grannie's argument.

Mercy shook her head. "I could tell how angry your grandfather was last night."

"He has a temper." Elspeth sighed. "So does Grannie. But she doesna show it lightly. Sometimes she just goes quiet." Elspeth didn't know how to explain that Grannie's silences were just as bad as Grandda's outbursts.

"Elspeth," Mercy said as she went back to work on the chicken, "it isn't my business to mind, but . . . what happened to your grannie's face? I've always wondered."

Elspeth sighed again, shrugging out of her shawl. The air was crisp and cool, and the sun soaking through the shoulders of her linsey-woolsey dress felt good. "Have ye heard Scots speak of The '45?" she asked. "England and Scotland share a king, you know. Thirty years ago, there was terrible fighting in Scotland because many Highlanders—those living in the northern part of Scotland, like my family—believed the wrong man sat on the throne. My family favored a prince, Charles Stuart, who was in exile in Europe. In 1745 Prince Charlie returned to Scotland and raised an army, mostly of Highlanders. My grandda joined his cause, and they set off to fight the British troops sent to defend the king."

"Ooh!" Mercy breathed. "Your grandfather said something last night about a battle. What was it?" She wrinkled her forehead.

Elspeth took a deep breath before forcing out the hated word. "Culloden. The Battle of Culloden was Prince Charlie's last. The Scottish Highlanders suffered a terrible defeat. Then the British killed many of the wounded Scotsmen as they lay bleedin' on the field. Some they didna kill outright but hanged later. And they sent some Scots off to the West Indies in ships, to be slaves."

Mercy gasped, shocked. "But—but your grandfather must have escaped."

"He did escape the battlefield. The prince did, too. Good folk helped the prince escape safe to France."

"What happened to your grandfather?"

"Grandda made his way home. He could no' live there, though. British soldiers searched everywhere for Highlanders who'd fought against them. Grandda hid in a cave for months. Then he was captured and put in prison for more than a year. The British finally let him go free, on his oath of loyalty. If he'd been captured right away, he'd likely be dead now, or gone for a slave."

"It's all so horrid!" Mercy stared at her wide-eyed.

"And after Culloden, British soldiers burned our houses and attacked women and turned children out to starve."

"Did the soldiers hurt your grannie?"

Elspeth hesitated. "Yes, but . . . but I canna say more."

Grannie's stories were hers, and rarely told. It was as if the memories were so painful that the old woman had built a wall around them, sealing them away. Elspeth couldn't speak of them—even to her best friend—without violating a trust. Besides, she could never truly make Mercy understand what the Battle of Culloden had meant to the Highland people.

Mercy looked thoughtful. "Elspeth, I don't understand. After everything your grandparents lived through, I would think they'd be eager to join the Patriot cause. The Patriots are fighting the same British government that caused the Highland Scots so much grief!"

Elspeth sighed. "The men feel torn in two, mostly. They ken it is no' so simple a task to rise against the British Crown." When Mercy frowned, Elspeth searched impatiently for the English word. "They understand, aye? And they know what can come from losing such a war. As for my grandda, he'll make up his own mind. He'll be pushed to it by nae man."

"What's all this?" Mistress Blair called cheerfully as she turned in the front gate. "You two look gloomy for such a fine day."

Elspeth jumped to her feet. "Good day, Mistress." She offered the kale. "Grannie sent these greens."

Mistress Blair was a little wren of a woman, brown-haired and energetic. When she smiled, as she did now, it reached straight into Elspeth's heart. "That will make

a lovely addition to supper, will it not, Mercy? Come
inside, girls. There's work to be done."

Aside from a table and benches near the fireplace,
the lower level of the Blairs' two-story home had been
given over to the business of producing cloth: two spin-
ning wheels, three looms, a pegged board for measuring
the long warp threads, baskets of fleece. The room
smelled faintly of raw wool and the urine that Mistress
Blair sometimes used to set the color of her dyes. Elspeth
felt completely at home there.

"Oh, a new one!" she breathed, darting to examine
the coverlet panel growing on the big eight-harness loom.
Mistress Blair was creating a bold pattern in red and blue
against the warp, or lengthwise threads, of cream wool.

Mistress Blair joined her at the loom. "I finished thread-
ing out the pattern yesterday. I call it 'Pine Bough'."

"It's lovely." Elspeth touched the cloth. "I do so like
the colors. And the design feels well balanced."

Mistress Blair smiled again. "Ah, Elspeth," she said.
"You have a weaver's heart."

For the next few hours Elspeth forgot about trouble.
While Mercy began stewing the chicken, Elspeth returned
to the four-harness loom in the corner where she'd been
working on a coverlet.

The simplest looms had only two treadles and created plain weave—cloth with no fancy pattern. Mistress Blair and Elspeth liked more complicated designs called overshot weaving, which required a loom with at least four treadles. Stepping on the treadles in a particular order, two at a time, caused certain threads to rise. That formed the path through which a weaver passed her wooden shuttles, which held the crosswise threads used to create the pattern.

Elspeth slid onto the bench, kicked off her shoes, and picked up her shuttles. She was using wool dyed a rich brown with walnut hulls to create a design against a white wool background. Soon her stockinged feet were sliding back and forth over the treadles, which had been worn shiny-smooth from use. After a few passes with the shuttles, she found her rhythm, the pattern echoing silently in her head: *2–3, 3–4, 1–4, 1–4* . . . The beater bar thumped as she pushed each woven thread into place on her loom, and the treadles clattered quietly. The smell of chicken stew filled the room.

When late afternoon sunlight slanted across the floor, Mistress Blair sighed, put her own shuttles aside, and stretched. "I believe I'll go fetch your father home from the tavern," she told Mercy. There were several taverns in Cross Creek, all popular meeting places for men with time to spare, and Mr. Blair often visited one or another to catch up on news. "Daughter, did you finish the bread?

Ah, good. You should have time to weave off that linen before I'm back. I promised it by tomorrow."

After her mother left, Mercy made a face. "I do hate linen," she sighed, sliding onto the bench at the smallest loom.

"If ye took a mind to fancy weaving, the boring work wouldna fall so much to you," Elspeth observed.

Mercy shook her head. "You know I can't keep the patterns straight. I always end up with skips and uneven edges."

Elspeth felt a wee bit sorry for Mistress Blair, who'd borne four children that lived, and none with her weaver's heart. Mercy was no use for anything but plain weave, and her three older brothers—all gone from home now— had no talent at the looms either. Still, if any of the Blair children *had* taken to weaving, Elspeth wouldn't be needed. That didn't bear thinking of.

And *that* thought brought back her other worries. "Mercy," she said, "about last night—remember how that Patriot called my grandda by name? He somehow knew we'd be bringin' ye home. Grandda said we'd been betrayed."

Mercy stilled her shuttle. "What do you mean?"

"Someone at the Gunns' *céilidh* sent the Patriots out for us."

"But who would do such a thing? I mean—all the people there besides me were Scottish, weren't they?"

Elspeth smoothed over a nubbin in her wool. "Scots dinna all think alike," she pointed out. "Remember that girl we met by the table, Jennet MacRacken? Grannie told me to stay away from her. I think there's some old argument between MacKinnons and MacRackens. Bad blood, Grannie said."

"You think the MacRackens are Patriots?" Mercy asked.

"I dinna know. Besides, Jennet said they were just come to this country."

"Even if they *are* Patriots, how would they—or anyone else—have known where to find us last night?"

Elspeth sighed. "Likely one of the people gathered round as we said good-bye told them. Grandda said clear and loud that he could no' meet with the lads that night, for taking ye home."

"Couldn't it have been anyone at the gathering?" Mercy cocked her head. "They all knew I'd come with you."

"Aye," Elspeth admitted. "But only those who heard Grandda speak would be sure we were no' planning to have ye spend the night with us. If ye had, we wouldna have been on the road where those Patriots were waiting."

"But if it *was* someone still at the party when we left, how could he have gotten word to the Patriots so quickly?"

"Perhaps one of the Patriots was skulkin' in the woods, just a-waiting," Elspeth said. "He'd have had time to hear the news and circle about, since we stopped at our cabin first."

Mercy fingered the woven fabric in front of her, looking troubled. "Well, I *suppose* so. What is your grandfather going to do?"

"I dinna know." Grandda had made it clear that he could not be bullied. He might think that was the end of it. But Elspeth could not forget what happened. Would more trouble make Grannie change her mind and keep Elspeth home?

Mercy stepped on a treadle and threw the shuttle through the open path. "Perhaps nothing serious will come of it. No one was hurt last night, after all. It was rather an adventure, don't you think?"

Elspeth was relieved that Mistress Blair's arrival spared her from answering. As Mercy's father settled by the hearth with his pipe, Mistress Blair invited Elspeth to stay to supper. "Thank you, I will," she said gratefully.

But Mercy's question echoed in her head. An adventure? Elspeth couldn't look at the exchange in the dark forest that way. Still, she was glad Mercy could. Mercy and her parents—they didn't *know,* in their bones, what war was. And because they did not, Elspeth could hide from the world in the crowded Blair home and pretend—just for a wee while—that it was her own.

CHAPTER 3
NOT CONTENT WITH THREATS

"So, Elspeth, how goes your work with the weaver?" Aunt Mary asked.

"Why, very well." Elspeth paused to skim a seed from the kettle of scuppernong grape jam she was stirring over the fire outside Aunt Mary's cabin. Golden rays of November sun slanted across the clearing, and the air was cool and dry.

"I've quite a bit of wool from our last shearing," Maggie Gunn said thoughtfully. "Perhaps enough for a coverlet. Or perhaps I'll just ask for a cradle blanket." Maggie was a plain girl with a round face and a quick smile. Only four years older than Elspeth, she was married and soon to be a mother.

"Mistress Blair weaves the loveliest patterns you can imagine," Elspeth told her.

Maggie's fingers stilled on the grapes she was plucking from their stems. "I was thinking I'd like *you* to weave it for me."

"I've much to learn yet," Elspeth said quickly. She didn't want to appear prideful to the little group of neighbor ladies who'd gathered to tend to the grape harvest.

Aunt Mary frowned. "I worry. Sending the girl in to Cross Creek—"

"Elspeth is learning a trade," Grannie said firmly. "There's no harm to come from that."

"This kettle is ready to pull from the fire," Elspeth announced, hoping to distract her aunt. Jings! Almost three weeks had passed since the night of the Gunns' *céilidh*, with no more trouble directly touching her family or their neighbors. Elspeth didn't need Aunt Mary to raise new concerns about Elspeth's work with the Blairs.

Elspeth helped her aunt lift the kettle from the trammel hook. When the jam cooled, they would ladle it into crocks to be sealed with wax and stored away. "That batch is done," Aunt Mary said. "I'll spread a noonday meal now. Child, run and let the boys know, aye?"

"Aye!" Elspeth nodded eagerly. The aroma of simmering grapes had made her hungry.

Aunt Mary's husband Gavin had died in a hunting accident soon after arriving in North Carolina. Duncan and Robbie, Elspeth's cousins, had begun the long process of wrestling fields from the forest by hacking a ring of bark from each tree, which caused the tree to die and drop its leaves. Without leaves in the way, sunlight reached the crops planted around the trees. So many dead trees gave

the field a spooky look and made it necessary for the men
to labor with hoes instead of plows. But over the coming
years, her cousins would gradually remove the trees.

Elspeth found Duncan and Robbie clearing the season's
last corn from the field behind the house. Duncan came
bounding like a doe when she waved. "I'm hollow as a
butter churn!" he exclaimed. "We thought you women had
forgotten to feed us."

Elspeth snorted. "You'd not suffer in silence overlong,
I think."

Duncan was a wiry boy of sixteen, with long dark curls
that tended to escape the leather thong he used to tie them
behind his neck. Elspeth admired how his spirit spilled
free too, from the grinding chores and the family heartaches and the looming fear of political troubles that had
squeezed the joy from the rest of her family. Now, although
his sweat-stained shirt hinted at a morning's hard labor,
he grinned and swung Elspeth nearly off the ground in an
exuberant dance. "There's nothing to come from suffering
in silence," he said as he set her down. He shot her a grin
and sauntered ahead to the cabin.

Robbie followed more slowly, and Elspeth waited for
him. "Elspeth, it's good to see you here," he said.

Elspeth hesitated. Ever since the night of the Gunns'
céilidh, she had been hoping for a moment alone with
Robbie. He had shouldered most of the burden since his
father had died. At nineteen he was taller than Duncan,

and thinner, with a face as sharp as a hatchet. Being near Duncan made Elspeth feel happier, and Robbie's quiet calm always made her feel safe.

"Robbie . . . I've been wanting to talk to you. Do you know any of the MacRackens?"

"No."

"I met a girl named Jennet MacRacken at the *céilidh*, and I've seen her at church since." Elspeth hated remembering how uncomfortable she'd felt in the churchyard, pinched between Jennet's friendly smile and Grannie's stern gaze. "But Grannie said I was to keep clear of her. Something about bad blood there. When I asked about it, Grannie got fierce angry."

"I know nothing of that, lass."

"Well, do you have any idea who sent the Patriots after us when Grandda and I took Mercy home?" Elspeth chewed her lower lip. "I think it must have been someone at the *céilidh*—someone who overheard Grandda tell you where we were headed."

Robbie looked sharply at her for a moment, then stared off at the forest as if seeing something far away. Finally he shook his head. "I don't recall who was standing near. But I'll not forget what happened to you." Then his grim expression softened, and he cocked his head toward the cabin. "Come along, before Duncan scrapes the pot clean."

Inside the cabin they found Grannie and Aunt Mary setting out platters of bass and duck and a basket of corn-

meal hoecakes besides, served with blackberry preserves.
The ladies sat at the table, and the boys crouched com-
fortably on the floor, heaping plates in hand.

"God save us," Aunt Mary scolded Duncan mildly.
"You eat like two men."

"I need my strength for the trip to Petersburg."
Duncan reached for another hoecake. "We hope to leave
in the morning."

"Petersburg!" Maggie Gunn looked startled. "All the
way to Virginia?"

"It's a long trip to Petersburg," Robbie acknowledged.
"But we've some fine corn and wheat, and a dozen head
of cattle to herd, too. If we take our goods and stock all
the way ourselves, we'll get a higher price. Why pay someone in Cross Creek to take barrels of grain and salt meat
downriver on flatboats when we can sell direct ourselves?"

"We already owe half of our profits to the landlord,"
Duncan added.

"I don't like it." Aunt Mary pinched her lips together,
and Elspeth could see that this was not a new discussion.
"These are troubled times. With you so long on the
road—"

"There's not a highwayman anywhere could take me
and Robbie!" Duncan's smile made his boast endearing
instead of annoying.

"The risk is small," Robbie said more quietly, "compared
to the profit."

Elspeth twiddled her spoon in her fingers, watching the long look exchanged between her aunt and Robbie. When her husband died, Aunt Mary hadn't turned bitter and angry like Grannie. Instead, she'd just . . . just emptied out, like a milkweed pod once its seeds dance away.

"Mary, you'll come stay with us while the boys are gone," Grannie decreed, getting up to check the fire. "They'll be home again soon enough."

"And we'll be that much closer to buying our own land!" Duncan cried. He jumped to his feet, grabbed his grandmother by the hand, and led her round the table in a gentle jig. "And then we'll be fine folks, with nothing to do but dance all day!"

Elspeth caught her breath at his daring, but Grannie actually smiled. Elspeth grinned, letting a wave of laughter and Gaelic talk wash over her. She knew how Robbie and Duncan ached to buy their own land. They were a long way from achieving their dream. Yet Robbie's quiet strength and Duncan's high-spirited determination made her believe that anything was possible.

At church that Sunday, Elspeth avoided Jennet's hopeful gaze as the families took their places in the pews. Instead of listening to the catechism, Elspeth found her mind tumbling around Grannie's unexplained dislike of the MacRackens. What had happened between them? While Grandda and Grannie and Aunt Mary bowed their heads, she dared a stealthy peek over her shoulder at Jennet and her father—

And froze.

Jennet was bent in prayer. But Tall Tam MacRacken was staring straight at Elspeth. The hard look in his eyes shocked her. Pressure from Grannie's elbow made Elspeth turn back to the front and bow her head, but the hairs on the back of her neck prickled for the rest of the service. When the final "Amen" was said and the congregation began to flow outside, she stayed close to her grandparents. She was grateful that the political troubles and disagreements kept people from lingering overlong after service as they used to do.

"Grandda," she whispered while Grannie and Aunt Mary walked ahead to ask how Maggie Gunn was feeling.

"What's that, lass?"

Elspeth took a deep breath. "Did ye know the MacRackens before they moved to North Carolina? That tall man over there?"

Grandda shook his head. "I only met him at the Gunns' *céilidh.*"

No help there. Elspeth set her jaw. Somehow or another, she'd sort this out.

The next morning, Aunt Mary helped Elspeth haul water for laundry. Elspeth waited for a quiet moment, out of earshot of the house, and asked her aunt about Grannie and the MacRackens.

Aunt Mary's forehead wrinkled in thought as she stooped to let a bucket fill with creek water. "Your grannie has a long memory," she said finally. "But it's not my tale to tell."

So, Aunt Mary *did* know why Grannie disliked the MacRackens! It must be a terrible story indeed, since Elspeth had never heard whisper of it before. *A long memory* ... Did the story stretch all the way back to The '45, the bitter time when British soldiers had rained cruelties upon the Highland people after the terrible battle at Culloden? "But can you just tell me —"

"It's your grannie's tale to tell," Aunt Mary repeated firmly. She hung a second full bucket from the yoke on Elspeth's shoulders and shooed her back toward the yard.

Elspeth's cousins returned from Petersburg one fine, sunny morning in early December. Elspeth was in the yard spooning myrtle berries into a kettle of boiling water and skimming off the waxlike material that rose to the surface, to be saved for candlemaking. Aunt Mary and Grannie were inside the cabin cooking, leaving Elspeth alone with her thoughts. She was trying to design a weaving draft in her head. She wanted to make Mistress Blair proud —

A shout interrupted her progress. Her cousins strode grimly into the yard. One of Robbie's eyes was purple and blue and swollen shut. Stains on Duncan's shirt told of a bloody nose.

Elspeth's sense of contentment plunged away. "What happened?" she cried.

"Is Grandda here?" Robbie asked, wincing. Blood was crusted on a gash in his lower lip.

Elspeth managed to swallow her questions. "I'll fetch him from the barn. Go on inside."

When she and Grandda hurried into the cabin, Robbie was seated by the window, being tended by his mother. "Last night, Grandda," Robbie managed, "we were visited on the road by Patriots about ten miles east of Cross Creek. Much like you were, only—"

"Only they weren't content with threats!" Duncan stalked across the room. "They wanted us to sign papers swearing loyalty to their cause."

Elspeth began to tremble.

"And did you sign?" Grandda asked, his face tight with anger.

"We did not," Robbie said, while Duncan exploded, "There's no man can tell us what to do! Why, I—"

"Will they be coming for you?" Aunt Mary interrupted sharply. "Was blood let?"

"No more than you see, on either side." Robbie winced again.

Elspeth saw the fear in her aunt's eyes and knew that she was remembering all the old tales from Scotland. Grannie's expression was as hard as stone.

"Grandda, there's more," Robbie said. "Those Patriots— I did not know a man of the lot. Nor did Duncan." He sighed, slumping back in the chair. "But they called us by name. Those Patriots *knew* we'd be on that road."

Elspeth heard a jay squawking from a pine tree outside. *Elspeth, lass, we were betrayed,* Grandda had said. Now someone had betrayed their family again. But who? Was it Tall Tam MacRacken?

Grannie's voice finally broke the stillness. "Hang the kettle on, Elspeth, and fetch up some bread."

The simple tasks eased Elspeth's nerves. When the family gathered around the table, Elspeth was able to keep her hands from quivering as she served up the platters.

"Angus." Grannie locked steel gazes with her husband. "It's time you decided which path this family will take."

Grandda put down his pewter tankard and wiped his mouth with the back of his hand. "I will," he said finally. "In my own time. Now, boys, what else came of your trip?"

Duncan told all the other news: their successful haggling for good prices, a fine roan mare he'd seen for sale . . . and something else. "This is not common known," he said, lowering his voice as if Patriots might be lurking at the door. "We met a man from Skye who'd heard that the British are sending two officers to recruit soldiers in

North Carolina—Brigadier General Donald MacDonald and Colonel Donald MacLeod."

Scottish names, both of them. *The British want the Scots as badly as the Patriots do,* Elspeth thought. She was suddenly desperate to be gone.

"I need to leave for Mistress Blair's," she murmured to Grannie.

Grannie nodded. "There's a bite in the air," she said. "Fetch the *arisaid* from the trunk."

Elspeth made a face as she knelt by the big wooden trunk in the corner and fetched the *arisaid*—a long length of heavy wool, cream with plum-colored stripes. It was old and showed signs of wear. And it was so *Scottish,* not like Mercy Blair's lovely winter cloak, which was lined and had a hood. Elspeth belted the *arisaid* around her waist so that one end hung to her ankles. She pulled the other end up over her shoulders and pinned it at her throat.

As she stepped into the yard, Duncan slipped outside after her. "Elspeth? You're off to Cross Creek? Be careful."

"Could it be you were mistaken?" she couldn't help asking. "Could it just have been thieves who set upon you?"

"They weren't after our shillings."

Elspeth nodded and squared her shoulders. Nothing was to be gained by pretending.

"Do you ever run errands for Mistress Blair?" Duncan asked.

"From time to time, to deliver a finished piece or

fetch some wool. Once to the apothecary for cochineal."
Cochineal was used to produce a lovely red dye.

"MacLeod's apothecary?" Duncan frowned, absently
rubbing the swollen knuckles on his right hand. "Murdock
MacLeod has been in the colony for many years. Some of
those Highlanders in Cross Creek, the merchants and such,
they're not like us. They're more English than not, and
likely Patriot. I don't want you coming to harm—"

"I won't," Elspeth interrupted, her fear of being kept
home outweighing her fear of the Patriots. "Grandda says
I may keep going, and Grannie—"

"I know." He sighed. "Well, don't speak of our troubles
with anyone. And if you're in Cross Creek and see a crowd
gathered near the print shop, or hear someone shouting
news, go the other way. And don't go to any taverns, especially the Black Bull. I'm told it's a rebel tavern. Sure to
be full of Patriots—"

"Duncan, now why would I go to a tavern in Cross
Creek?"

He looked startled, then laughed sheepishly, shoving
one long curl back from his forehead. "Aye, you're right.
But know this." The laughter died from his eyes. "If anyone ever frightens you, or speaks to you roughly, I'll see
he lives to regret it." His fingers curled into a fist. "Away
with you, now."

CHAPTER 4
THE STRANGER IN THE WOODS

Mr. Blair greeted Elspeth at the door. "Mercy is visiting her brother's wife," he told her. "Polly's cleaning her flax crop and needs some help. And my wife isn't feeling well. She's upstairs resting. But she said you would know what needed doing."

"Aye, sir, that I do." Elspeth settled at her loom. The pattern draft hung from a nail, and she'd poked a pin at the spot where she'd stopped. But worry nibbled at her concentration, and she struggled to find her rhythm.

Who had sent the Patriots again? *Who?* One of the women who'd helped preserve the grape harvest at Aunt Mary's might have mentioned the boys' trip to her husband, or perhaps the boys had told their friends ... Elspeth shook her head. There were too many possibilities.

But why had Angus MacKinnon and his grandsons been singled out? Was it only because her grandfather

was a respected man among the Scottish working folk?
Or was it something more—

Elspeth started when a hand dropped on her shoulder.
"Oh—Mr. Blair! I didna notice ye come."

"What's troubling you, Elspeth?" he asked kindly. "I
usually love to hear the beater bar come home and the
treadles rattle. But not today. You're not in swing."

"I've a thing or two on my mind," Elspeth confessed,
feeling her face grow warm. "But I'll set to, right away."

Mr. Blair fingered the woven yardage wrapping around
the front beam, reminding Elspeth that he had for many
years supported his family by weaving fine linen and wool
cloth. "He taught Mama," Mercy had told her. "And Mama
took to it." Mistress Blair had taken over the business as
her husband's eyes grew cloudy, and she had made it her
own by specializing in overshot patterns. But Mr. Blair
had not forgotten his craft, even if he could no longer see
one thread against the next.

"You do fine work," he said, his fingers moving over
the cloth. "Your edges are trim. I have no patience for a
weaver who can't weave a straight edge. But here—" His
fingers stopped an inch or so below the last thread Elspeth
had beaten into place. "This is where you began today,
I think. This last bit isn't even. The tension is off."

Elspeth's shoulders slumped. He was right, and Mistress
Blair expected better of her. "'Tis rare sorry I am," she said
miserably. "I'll pull it out and do it over."

"That'll do fine, child. Not to worry. You're a blessing to my family, don't you know that?"

Tears stung Elspeth's eyes. "Thank you," she whispered.

"Before you get back to the shuttles, would you walk to town with me? I'll spend the afternoon with a pint and some good talk."

Mo chreach! Elspeth sat up straight. The very day Duncan warned her against going to a tavern, Mr. Blair wanted her to do just that! "Oh—aye, Mr. Blair," she faltered. "Where will ye be wantin' to go for that pint?"

"They serve a fine rum toddy at the Two Sisters." Mr. Blair made his way back through the maze of looms toward the door. The women were always careful not to rearrange anything.

Elspeth gulped with relief as she slipped on her shoes and reached for her wrap. For a moment she had been afraid that Mercy's father might want to go to the Black Bull. But—wait! Perhaps . . . perhaps if she happened to walk past the Black Bull on her way back to the Blairs' house, she'd see someone she recognized going inside. A Scot. Maybe even Jennet MacRacken's father, Tall Tam.

The chance of something suspicious happening at the very moment she passed the Patriot tavern was, Elspeth realized, very small. And, sure enough, when she paused beneath the tavern's wooden sign, nothing suspicious *did* happen. A young man with blond curls and a twig of pine tucked in his buttonhole nodded cheerfully at her as he went inside. An old peddler with a basket of goods on his back trudged past, using an upended broom as a walking stick. Nothing more.

At least I tried, Elspeth thought as she headed back to the Blair home. Just trying to learn more about whoever was frightening her family staved off her sense of helplessness. Duncan's warning echoed in her mind, and the memory of that night after the *céilidh* made her clench her teeth. But too much was at stake to hide behind her cousins. Hadn't she been raised on tales of a war that tore her family apart? If there was anything she could do to keep that from happening again, she would.

December slid into January. Worry hung in the air like smoke at the MacKinnons' cabin, and followed Elspeth even when she escaped to the Blairs' home.

"I dread whatever 'tis waiting to fall upon us," Elspeth confessed to Mercy one afternoon, when sleet rattled against the windows and Mistress Blair was resting upstairs again. Elspeth crouched behind her loom, checking the tension of her warp threads. "Whoever betrayed my family, twice now, is surely just bidin' his time for another chance."

Mercy sat by the hearth, carding wool. "Elspeth, you do worry! Can you not leave that to the men?"

"'Tis because I'm Scottish." Elspeth sighed, suddenly wishing with all her heart that she *weren't* Scottish, not even a wee bit. She was tired of living on old anger, tired of waiting for the next blow.

"Has there been more trouble?"

"None since my cousins'," Elspeth admitted. "But Grandda storms about when he's at chores, and Grannie is sore bad-tempered, too. Why, just this morn, she—" Elspeth stopped abruptly. She didn't want to tell Mercy how Grannie had reacted when Elspeth asked if she might stay the night with the Blairs if the weather didn't clear. "I want you home this night," she'd snapped. Elspeth had nodded quickly before scuttling away.

Mercy beckoned to Elspeth. "Come sit with me a moment. I've news to share."

Elspeth joined Mercy, glad enough to sit closer to the fire's warmth. "News of the rebellion?"

"No!" Mercy leaned close. "It's mother. She's with child again."

"With child?" This was news indeed! *She'll be needing me even more once the babe comes,* Elspeth thought.

"She doesn't wish to speak of it yet. She lost the two babes she tried to carry after me. But I know she won't mind me telling you." Mercy linked her arm through her friend's. "Just think, if all is well, we'll have a baby to tend come spring! Won't that be lovely?"

Elspeth was delighted that Mercy had wanted to share

the news with her—just as a sister would. "Lovely, indeed," she agreed, and smiled.

⬧

"Mistress Pigeon!" Mercy's mother greeted a sharp-chinned woman of middling age later that afternoon. "Do come in. That shirting cloth you ordered is ready."

Mercy had left to fetch her father home after her mother had risen from her nap. Elspeth stayed busy at her loom as Mistress Blair settled near the fire with her customer, and the hum of conversation was as lulling as the rhythmic clatter of the treadles. But suddenly Elspeth froze, straining to hear.

"...those *Scots*," Mistress Pigeon was saying. "Mr. Pigeon is afraid they're going to fight for the Loyalist cause. If so, they'll get their due! Mr. Pigeon says he can't understand how these newcomer Scots think. They come into the bakery sometimes. They're such peculiar people—"

"I haven't found that at all," Mistress Blair interrupted firmly. "My apprentice is from Scotland, and she's a dear."

Her face hot, Elspeth forced herself to thump the beater bar home.

"But...oh...I see," Mistress Pigeon faltered. "She doesn't speak much English, does she? I thought—"

"Elspeth speaks English very well." Mistress Blair gave her guest a calm smile. "Now, let's see about that shirting."

When Mistress Pigeon had left, Mercy's mother came to stand beside Elspeth. "Never mind," she said. "What's the word you use for speaking nonsense? Blethering? Mistress Pigeon blethers."

"Mistress Pigeon is a Patriot?"

"Her husband is. That's no secret in Cross Creek." Mistress Blair spread her hands. "I must take business from Loyalist and Patriot alike. I can't afford to turn away work."

Elspeth nodded slowly. Was Mistress Pigeon's husband one of the men who'd accosted Grandda? Elspeth stared at her hands. Was she weaving cloth for the very people who were frightening her family?

Although Elspeth was familiar with the several blocks that made up Cross Creek's business section, she had ventured inside any of the buildings only on rare errands for Mistress Blair or on even rarer shopping excursions with her grandparents. On these streets, travelers heading to Wilmington or Winston-Salem searched for a meal, and French or Welsh or German farmers shopped for supplies. Merchants wearing fine clothes had shops with big glass windows and brightly painted wooden signs. The strangeness of this place, and the people, made Elspeth uncomfortable.

That afternoon, however, she found her way to a shop with a sign she remembered, painted with a pigeon and a loaf of bread. She knew the freezing rain would slink through the *arisaid* and darkness would be upon her before she got home, even if she hurried. Still, she'd been used to winter rains on Skye, and she had business to attend to. Would poor weather have kept her mother from such a task?

When she peeked in the bakeshop window she saw no sign of Mistress Pigeon, so Elspeth took a deep breath and slipped inside. The room smelled wonderfully of bread and nutmeg and molasses. Elspeth couldn't help staring at crusty loaves of bread piled on the counter beside a variety of smaller baked goods she didn't recognize—rolls and buns and tiny flat wafers.

"These aren't fresh," a large woman was complaining to the shopgirl, poking a loaf of bread with an indignant finger. "Don't you have anything else?"

The girl, who looked tired, stepped to a side door and leaned outside. "Father? Do you have one more batch coming yet today?"

"I've got a dozen loaves of wheat bread in the last oven," a man's voice called. "They need more time yet."

Elspeth stiffened. *That* must be Mr. Pigeon—the baker, the Patriot, the man she had come to see. She hurried outside. She turned the corner and saw three brick bake ovens sheltered under an overhang in the lane beside the bakery.

There—the man in the flour-dusted apron—that must be Mr. Pigeon. He stood holding the huge paddle he used to retrieve baked loaves, the blackened blade resting on the ground between his feet, and was deep in conversation with a red-haired man. That man wore leather moccasins, a checked linen shirt over worn breeches, and a felt hat so old it had lost its shape.

Elspeth had only planned to learn what Mr. Pigeon looked like. Now she wanted to know what he and his friend were discussing. But how?

Nerves fluttering, she began to limp, then crouched under a corner of the overhang and fussed with her shoe as if she'd picked up a tiny stone.

Mr. Pigeon turned. "You there! What are you doing?"

Elspeth smiled politely and greeted the men in Gaelic.

The baker flapped his hand at her. "I don't speak that gabble tongue. Go on with you."

Elspeth slipped her shoe back on and straightened her knitted stocking as the red-haired man began speaking again. ". . . and just as he called 'Look at me, Papa!' he fell off the fence and landed in the hog pen!" Mr. Pigeon chuckled, and the storyteller laughed so hard that a tiny sprig of pine adorning his ridiculous hat bobbed up and down.

Elspeth moved on. Horrid Patriots! Rude to her because she spoke Gaelic. And that second man—wearing a pine twig for decoration! He didn't even realize how dark and depressing the endless pine forest in North Carolina was. He had probably never smelled salt air, or looked for starfish in tide pools, or heard seals bark, or walked in the sunshine by the sea.

Enough for today, she thought, fighting a wave of home-sickness. The wind carried needlelike pellets of sleet. As she circled back to the main street, she noticed spots of candlelight beyond thick windowpanes and wished that she were somewhere cozy, too.

A farm wagon rattled past, its wheels crunching in the icy ruts, but there was little traffic on the street. Walking with head bowed against the weather, Elspeth was startled when someone stepped from the apothecary's door into her path. "*Gabh mo lethsgeul!*" the girl said quickly. *Pardon me!*

Elspeth stopped short, recognizing Jennet MacRacken's speckled face peering from beneath her hood.

"Elspeth! Good afternoon! I came to town with my father. He's inside." Jennet cocked her head at the apothe-cary shop, then added shyly, "Elspeth . . . would you like to come to my house some time? We could share chores—perhaps sewing or fulling wool?"

"Jennet, did your family know mine back in Scotland? Maybe your grandparents?" Elspeth felt her face flush; she hadn't meant to be so direct! Still, if no one in her own family would tell her what "bad blood" stood between the MacRackens and the MacKinnons, maybe Jennet would.

But Jennet shook her head, looking puzzled. "I don't think so. Why?"

"It's nothing. Excuse me, but I need to be on my way."

"*Beannachd leat,*" Jennet said slowly, but Elspeth was

already turning away and didn't say good-bye in return. She felt as miserable as the weather.

"I *hate* all this trouble," she muttered. "Hate it, hate it, hate it!"

Elspeth left Cross Creek behind and found the forest path that would lead her home. Icy rain still beat upon her shoulders, but at least the hunting trail was sheltered by the towering trees. The air smelled of mud and pine. And the dusky light reminded her to hurry—

Then a shadow separated from a massive tree beside the path and planted itself in front of her.

Elspeth froze. The man before her seemed as tall as Robbie, but heavy-built. The rain and the shadows blurred his face and clothes, but his words were clear: "Elspeth Monro." It was an English voice, hard and cold.

Elspeth's heart began to thump in her chest. Her knees turned to oatmeal.

"Elspeth Monro!"

She scoured up every bit of her courage, trying to sound like Grandda. "I am. And who might ye be?"

"A Patriot."

"Well, that's of no account to me. I'll thank ye to step aside so I can be on my way." Elspeth licked her dry lips, noticing the glint of a pistol in the man's hand. She took a step to the side.

But the man quickly blocked her path. "I've a message for Angus MacKinnon."

Elspeth willed her voice not to tremble. "Then ye . . . ye need to be speakin' to him."

The man grabbed her shoulder, digging his fingers through the thick wool, and she yelped in pain. He pushed down until Elspeth's knees buckled and she sank to the path in front of him. She smelled the wet wool of his cloak. She saw the mud caked on his shoes.

"Your grandfather must declare his intentions," the man growled. "And he would be wise to choose for the Patriots. This is his final warning."

Elspeth's fear exploded into anger. "Are ye afeard to speak to Grandda direct, then?" she demanded, squinting up at him. "Ye coward! Who sent ye? Tell me that!"

But he released her shoulder and disappeared as suddenly as he had come, melting into the forest shadows.

For a moment, Elspeth remained on her knees. Her shoulder ached, and she still had the trembles. Tears burned her eyes and mingled with rain on her cheeks. Then she swiped the tears away angrily and stumbled to her feet. She brushed off her shoulder, wanting to wipe the stain of the Patriot's fingers from the wool.

Suddenly, a wave of warmth drove out the last of her shivers—as if the old Scottish *arisaid* was a warm hug about her shoulders. "I can stand up to the likes of you," she told the dark night. She fished her firesteel from her pocket and managed to light the candle in her lantern. Thus armed, she headed for home.

CHAPTER 5

DIFFICULT CHOICES

Elspeth sat hunched by the hearth that night while her grandparents argued. "This is not enough to set you to action, Angus MacKinnon?" Grannie demanded. "Elspeth herself set upon? You must declare yourself!"

"I have no need of you to say what I must do!"

"No." Grannie's voice was bitter. "It would humble a mighty man like you to take heed of his wife. God save us from your pride." She headed for the door. Elspeth opened her mouth as Grannie banged outside, but her grandfather motioned her to silence.

"But, Grandda, it's late and it's cold, and there may yet be Patriots about!"

"She's just gone to the barn, I think," Grandda said. "Let her grumble at the chickens. These walls do close in at times." For a long moment her grandfather stood still, lost in thought. Then he went to the trunk in one corner and rummaged inside. When he returned to the bench near the fire, he held a battered hat in his hands.

"I wore this bonnet marchin' off to join the prince for The '45," he said, staring at it.

"What's that?" Elspeth pointed at a limp cockade made from white ribbon sewn to the cap.

Grandda looked surprised. "Why, 'tis the white rose! White roses were the symbol of support for our own Prince Charlie. All the lasses wore them on their gowns, and we lads on our bonnets. It let folks know where we stood, aye? And those fightin' *against* the prince wore red or yellow crosses on their bonnets."

Elspeth shivered, imagining men struggling to distinguish friend from foe on the bloody battlefield at Culloden.

"'Tis an old custom. Men of different clans wore sprigs of certain plants in their hats to let others know who they faced." With a faint smile, Grandda tried the cap on for her. "Well, lass?"

"Ye still look fierce, Grandda," Elspeth said, and he looked pleased. But the talk of clan emblems reminded Elspeth of the pine twig bobbing from the hat of the baker's friend. And hadn't she noticed a sprig of pine in the buttonhole of a man going into the Black Bull? *If they were Scottish, I'd think they were of the same clan,* she thought.

But . . . wait. *Were* the pine twigs a sign? Had the Patriots adopted them as a signal of their allegiance? It must be so! Baker Pigeon was a Patriot, so likely his friend was, too. And likely the young man visiting the Black Bull was a Patriot.

What about Tall Tam MacRacken? Was Jennet's father sporting a pine sprig as well?

Jings! Now she had a clue to look for.

The next evening, Grandda's friends and neighbors began to arrive when chores were done, still smelling of cow and sweat. They came with sharp knives tucked into their stockings, or with pistols or muskets in hand. Almost two dozen crowded into the little cabin.

Alasdair MacKay, the piper, came with his father, Red John MacKay. Neill MacNeill arrived straight from the gristmill where he worked, chaff still dusting his hair. A handful of young men Elspeth recognized as friends of her cousins came, loud and restless. Grim-faced older men filed in silently. Most left their wives at home to mind children and hearth, but Aunt Mary came with Duncan and Robbie, and the Gunns came together.

Elspeth had baked hoecakes that afternoon, and as the men found places, she offered each a bite to eat. Her basket was almost empty when the door opened again and two men slid inside—Jennet MacRacken's father and uncle.

So, they came, Elspeth thought, staring at Tall Tam MacRacken. Was it coincidence that she'd been confronted by the Patriot so soon after meeting Jennet on the street in Cross Creek?

The two men settled in one corner. "Something to eat?" she asked, offering the basket. She heard the edge in her tone and was glad of it. This time Tall Tam didn't meet her gaze, and Elspeth felt a ripple of satisfaction. She looked both men over carefully but saw no telltale sprigs of pine.

Her responsibilities complete, Elspeth started toward the ladder to the loft, thinking to stay out of the way. Grannie put a hand on her arm. "*Elisaid,* stay," she ordered softly. "You've earned that right." *That I have,* Elspeth thought, and she settled down to listen.

Grandda stood near the hearth. "You've heard of the latest insult to my family," he began. "I've been of a mind to stay out of this trouble between the Patriots and the Loyalists. We're new come to the colonies, and I don't see it as my fight—"

"Grandda, they're *making* it our fight!" Duncan interrupted.

Grandda stilled Duncan with a stern gaze. "That may be. And this latest mischief against Elspeth has sore tried my patience. But there's more at stake here than what's to come to me and my own. The Patriots have as much as said that if I don't join their cause and bring some of you with me, they'll rain trouble down upon us. We're none of us safe. I'd like to hear what every man here has to say."

The hearthfire's crackle filled the sudden silence.

Elspeth watched the men look at each other, at their hands, back at Grandda. Long ago in Scotland, before The '45, clan chiefs had told their men who to fight and when to do it. The clan system was broken now, even in Scotland, and Grandda was not a chief. But Elspeth couldn't help wondering if some of these men wished he would simply tell them what to do. Grandda spoke English well, and he had survived the Battle of Culloden. Looking at her grand-father's fierce gaze, his proud posture, Elspeth knew why the others looked to him as a leader.

Finally Hector Gunn spoke up. "From what I've heard, the Patriots have fair complaints against the Crown," he said slowly. "We all know how cruel harsh the English can be. Still, I don't like much of what I see of the Patriots, either."

"They're rabble," another man agreed. "Skulking about at night."

Duncan jumped to his feet. "They're not honorable! Robbie and me set them to a run when they waylaid us, so they tried to put a fear into Elspeth. A wee girl! I'd like to take a broadsword and hunt down every—"

"Duncan, sit down." Robbie rolled his eyes, but Elspeth noticed a smile twitching the corners of his mouth.

Alasdair MacKay's fingers played along his thigh, as if wishing for his bagpipes. "I don't like how your family's been challenged," he said to Grandda. "Still, I see sense behind many of the Patriots' arguments, and I've no love for the English. But"—he paused, looking around the room—

"I can't see my way clear to join the Patriots. My grandda died at Culloden, and my grandmother soon after. We all know what happened. The British army is too powerful. I don't believe the Patriots can win."

Elspeth felt a shiver of the old fear. Her family knew well what happened to people who fought against the British army—and lost.

"Besides that," said Neill MacNeill, "my family's still in Scotland. What would the soldiers there do to my parents if I fought with the Patriots here in America?"

Maggie Gunn folded her hands over her belly as if shielding the babe growing within. "My Hector's got family to protect right here! The Patriots have already run the royal governor from the colony. Do you think we should heed the Patriots' warning, Angus?"

Grandda scratched his ear, looking sober. "I have searched my conscience, and I know that I cannot do what the Patriots ask. I cannot raise arms against the British. I swore an oath of loyalty to the British Crown."

"The royal governor says that any man who does not defend the king will stand to have his life and property taken," Duncan added, jabbing the air with his forefinger. "The governor's exiled on a ship now, but we know that he's working to take back control of the colony from the Patriots."

Neill shook his head stubbornly. "This is not my fight."

Robbie had been squatting against the wall, but he

stretched up to his full height now. "I say it's mine."

Aunt Mary made a tiny strangled noise in her throat.

"And why is that?" Neill asked.

Robbie spread his hands. "There's land to be had, man! *Land.* British officers promise that every man who fights for the king will get two hundred acres of land—and no taxes for twenty years after!"

A mutter rippled around the room. Elspeth saw the men's hunger. These were men who scratched a bare living from rented land or, if they were lucky, from small farms they called their own. More prosperous emigrants who had arrived on Elspeth's ship had claimed sprawling tracts further north and west of Cross Creek. These men, *her* men and their friends, had not been so fortunate.

The door banged open and a friend of Duncan's burst into the room. "I'm here from Cross Creek," he panted. "I heard a rumor this afternoon and stayed to make sure it was true—"

"Out with it, then," Grandda snapped.

"Governor Martin has this day issued a proclamation. He's called upon all loyal subjects to unite and crush the rebellion. Loyalist leaders in each county have been given authority to recruit militia, fix officers, and seize weapons and supplies from the Patriots—"

"I say we fight with the Loyalists!" Duncan cried. "For the king, and for land!" He'd worn his great plaid that evening, and his long dark curls spilled free. The fire in his eyes reminded Elspeth that his Gaelic name, *Donnchadh,* meant "brown warrior."

"We should raise a company," someone else yelled. "Angus can lead us!"

For a moment, Elspeth wanted to cheer. She *wanted* her cousins to fight against the man who'd forced her to kneel in fear before him. But one look at Grannie, sitting stone-faced nearby, stilled her fever. *She must feel like she's caught in a bad dream,* Elspeth thought. It was happening just as it had thirty years earlier—Grandda marching off to fight, Grannie left behind.

Some of the other men were on their feet, too, and the muster might have begun right there if Grandda's voice had not cracked across the commotion. "*No.*" He waited for silence. "I'll respect the choice of any man here. But," he said, glancing at his wife, "I am not ready to join the Loyalists. Me and *mine*"—he gave Duncan and Robbie a severe look—"will bide in peace a while longer."

Duncan blinked in disbelief. "Grandda—"

"Wheesht!" Grandda barked. "I've spoken my mind on this. But there is one thing more." He circled the room slowly, looking each man in the eye. "Three times, now, Patriots have insulted my family. They knew where to find us, and when to find us there. I am hard-pressed to explain how the Patriots would come by such information unless someone who knew my family's business well gave it to them. That man is likely in this room."

Elspeth couldn't help sneaking a look at Jennet's father. Had he chosen that corner spot, deep in the shadows, on purpose?

"You've heard me say that I'm not ready to raise my hand against either side in this American rebellion," Grandda said. "But hear this, too. If I find the man responsible for threats against my family, by God I'll raise my hand and more."

The room was so still that Elspeth heard a mouse rustling in the loft.

Grandda crossed his arms. "And what was said here this night goes no farther. I'll have no man come to harm because he spoke his mind under my roof. Aye?"

"Aye," the men echoed, glancing uneasily at each other. "Aye."

Grandda nodded, satisfied. "Elspeth," he called, "fetch round a stirrup cup."

After Elspeth had served each guest a drink for the road, the men wrapped themselves well against the wind and left for home. As they headed out, a few continued the debate in groups of two or three. Elspeth managed to stand near Jennet MacRacken's father and uncle as they left. "So, what do you think?" Tall Tam muttered to his brother, but the men were outside before she heard any more.

Duncan, Robbie, and Aunt Mary lingered. The family gathered around the table, and the boys tried one more time to convince Grandda to join the Loyalist cause.

More arguments, more anger, Elspeth thought wearily.

Robbie said his piece and grew silent, but Duncan couldn't let go. "Then let us fight, Grandda, if you don't want to raise a company yourself. Robbie and I can fight—"

Elspeth saw Grandda's face growing red and braced for the explosion. Instead, Grannie suddenly stretched out her good arm and swept pewter plates and mugs to the floor with a resounding clatter. "*Enough!*" she snapped into the shocked silence. "You boys don't know what war is."

"I've heard enough tales," Duncan said stubbornly.

"And I say, you—don't—know!" Grannie's glare defied his argument. "You didn't live through it. You're no blood of mine if you dare scorn your grandda for not joining in now."

For a long moment, no one spoke. Finally Robbie stood up. "You're right, Grannie, we weren't there," he said quietly. "Come, Duncan. We should get Mother home."

Elspeth's cousins and aunt left in silence. Grandda stalked off to the woodpile to vent his own frustration. Elspeth cleaned up the mess on the floor and banked the fire. Still her grandmother hadn't moved. Elspeth didn't like the look in her eyes.

"Come, Grannie," she tried. "Let me help you get ready for bed. Shall I comb out your hair?"

They sat on the edge of the bed. Elspeth took off the white cap Grannie wore during the day and began working free the untidy coil hidden beneath it.

"I once had beautiful hair." Grannie's voice sounded far away.

"You still do." Elspeth thought Grannie's hair, a mix of smoke gray and iron gray and white, was a glory.

"That was before the British soldiers came."

Elspeth's hand suddenly clenched on the comb. She should have known the night's arguments might set off one of Grannie's spells.

"The soldiers came looking for the men, for the Highlanders who'd fought against them at Culloden. But the men were all gone, dead or hiding or in prison. So they made war on the women and children."

"I know, Grannie."

"The first time they came for Angus, I let them search the place. But that wasn't enough. They dragged me outside, six of them—"

"You've told me this before!" Elspeth wanted to clap her hands over her ears.

"—and I could hear my children crying the whole time. Peggy screamed 'Don't hurt my mother!' over and over, and her just ten years old. She always was a bold one."

Peggy. Elspeth felt her own twist of loss, picturing the mother she had never known.

"When the soldiers marched off, my right arm was so badly hurt, I knew I'd never use it again, nor my hand. I can't remember clear, but I think the officer, him that was mounted, caused his horse to step on it."

Elspeth took a deep breath and began to ply the comb again. "It was a terrible time," she said carefully. "But that was long ago, Grannie. Back in Scotland. I don't think such things will happen here in North Carolina." When Grannie didn't answer, Elspeth came around to crouch on the floor in front of her. "Grannie? Grannie!"

The old woman blinked. "What? Peggy, is that you?"

Elspeth swallowed hard. "No, it's Elspeth, Peggy's daughter. Elspeth, remember?"

"Elspeth? Yes, yes, I remember." Grannie stared at her granddaughter, then took her hand. "I shouldn't have spoken. You must never repeat these stories, child. These memories should die with me. The burden must be mine alone."

By the time Grandda came back inside, Elspeth had helped Grannie into bed and had climbed to her own pallet in the loft. She heard Grandda slide the latch into place and throw another log on her carefully banked fire. That meant he'd sit up late, staring at the flames and facing his own memories with a dram or two of whisky.

Elspeth lay awake, too, watching the twisting shadows thrown by the firelight against the ceiling and thinking back on the evening. Several men had expressed understanding for the Patriot cause, but none had spoken forcefully for it. And no one had worn a pine sprig. As for Tall Tam, he had remained silent.

How could she learn more about him? She knew so

little. He attended Presbyterian services at MacKay's Meeting House, and he helped his brother operate a gristmill. He had visited the apothecary in Cross Creek at least once, because she had bumped into Jennet while he was inside. Murdock MacLeod, who owned that shop, was Scottish too—but one of the "old Scots," men who'd settled in the area years earlier and prospered, and now appeared more English than not, to the newcomers' way of thinking. *They're likely Patriots,* Duncan had said.

Well, next time she went to Cross Creek, she would visit the apothecary shop.

At least tonight she'd been able to stop Grannie before the old woman's memories had moved on to the last time the British soldiers came looking for Grandda. That cold day, when she'd marched outside to face them, they'd thrown a torch onto the thatched roof of the stone cottage. Grannie's face had been burned as she tried to get her five children out safe. That she'd done, but two had starved in the long months that came after.

Could the same thing happen again? Here, in North Carolina? Elspeth didn't know. All she *did* know was that someone, someone close to the family, was making things worse than they already were.

CHAPTER 6

UNEXPECTED DISCOVERY

The next day, over a midday meal of potato soup, Grandda eyed Elspeth. "You've said little about what happened to you in the woods, lass. Do you want to give up your work and stay home?"

The prospect of traveling alone in the woods again made Elspeth's stomach churn. But the thought of giving up her time with the Blairs—even after all that had happened, that still felt worse. "I wish to keep on with my work," she said.

Grandda nodded. "I thought you would. But wait for me or one of your cousins to walk you home at day's end."

"Oh, thank you, Grandda." Elspeth felt a rush of relief.

"Meet at Clear Spring," Grandda said. "Be there before full dark, aye?"

Grannie waited until her husband went outside before speaking. "You made the right choice, *Elisaid*. Away with you, now. Hang some water over the fire to heat before you go, and I'll clean up."

While Elspeth hung the iron kettle over the fire, Grannie poured some dried beans into a large linen napkin to send along to the Blairs. "Let me help you with that," Elspeth offered when she turned and saw Grannie trying to knot all four corners of the napkin over the beans—no easy task with only one good hand.

"I can manage!" Grannie flared. Elspeth knew better than to argue. Instead she fetched the *arisaid* from its peg, trying to keep her hurt feelings and worries from showing.

Grannie's expression softened as she put the package into a basket and handed it to Elspeth. "You'll do fine, child. You do mind me of your mother." She gave a faint smile. "Especially when you wear that."

"This *arisaid*?"

"It was hers, you know. Peggy's."

Elspeth blinked. "It *was*?" How could she not have known that? She caught her breath, remembering the comfort she'd taken from the wrap after the Patriot had accosted her in the woods. She fingered the thick woolen cloth reverently. It didn't seem so old and musty anymore.

"Let it keep you safe. You must be strong like your mother was, Elspeth. Don't give up your trade, no matter what comes. I want you to be able to earn your own way in the world, so promise me that."

"I promise, Grannie," Elspeth said solemnly. "That I do."

Before leaving for the Blairs', Elspeth took a wooden bucket to the creek to get water for her grandmother. The day was clear and cold, with only weak sun trying to poke through the trees, but Grannie's words warmed her. *Grannie can be so kind,* Elspeth thought as she started slowly back up the narrow path to the cabin. *If only she'd let that side show more often.* Elspeth had always hated Grannie's anger, but after her own experience in the woods with the Patriot, she thought she understood it better. Maybe living on anger was better than living on fear—

Elspeth's thoughts died abruptly, and her body went rigid. Ahead of her, by the main trail, a man stood beside an enormous pine tree. He appeared to be watching the MacKinnon cabin. Wearing a tricorn hat and a brown coat and breeches, he was almost invisible in the shadows. Only the harsh outline of the musket in his hand had caught Elspeth's attention. Elspeth couldn't see the man's face, but he was very tall and very thin.

Tall Tam MacRacken.

Was he trying to learn if Grandda had answered the Loyalists' call to arms? What should she do? Grandda was in the barn, but she'd have to pass Tall Tam to get there. Elspeth hesitated, considering. Her fingers began to cramp, and very slowly she eased the heavy bucket to the ground.

When she straightened again, Tall Tam had disappeared.

Elspeth ran to the barn. "Grandda!" she cried breathlessly as she plunged inside. "I just saw a man standing by the trail. I think it was Tall Tam MacRacken!"

Grandda tossed a shovelful of dirty straw from the cow's stall. "And what of it?"

"He—he was watching the cabin! And carrying a gun!"

Grandda leaned on his shovel and regarded her with a frown. "Nae doubt the man was out hunting, lass. Just trying to feed his family."

"But . . ." Elspeth's voice trailed away. She didn't know how to make Grandda understand. She thought for a moment, then tried again. "Grandda, I know that a few Scots fought for the British king during The '45 back in Scotland, instead of against him, as you did."

"Aye, that's so."

"Did the MacRackens fight for the king?"

He pitched more soiled straw from the stall. "No, lass, not that I can say. 'Twas the Campbells and their ilk, mostly. I didna hear of a MacRacken doin' so."

So much for her idea that Grannie harbored an old grudge against Jennet's family because they had fought for the wrong side thirty years earlier.

Elspeth stewed all the way to Cross Creek, but at least she didn't see Tall Tam or any Patriots lurking in the woods. Mercy came skipping outside when Elspeth approached. "We missed you yesterday," she cried. "Mother told me not to fret, but I think she was worried, too."

"'Tis sorry I am for that," Elspeth said with a sigh. "I needed to help Grannie with some extra baking, and

I didna have any way to send word." Elspeth quickly told her friend about meeting the Patriot in the woods and about the gathering Grandda had called at their cabin.

Mercy looked horrified. "I would have been too frightened to gather my wits!"

"I *was* frightened," Elspeth said slowly. "But when he pushed me down on the ground, then I got angry, too. That helped."

The two girls went inside, and Elspeth felt the worry slide from her shoulders. Mercy was baking, and the room smelled of yeast and rye. This frame house was much brighter than her own dark cabin. No one here lived on old sorrows. No one here was stalked by threatening Patriots or being watched. Mr. Blair was almost blind—of no use to either Patriot or Loyalist. *I'm safe here,* Elspeth thought. She wished she could stay forever.

Mistress Blair's loom was empty, and she needed Elspeth's help winding the yards and yards of lengthwise warp threads onto the back beam. It was tricky business, for if the threads tangled, the weaver would not be able to throw her shuttle with ease. But it was one of a weaver's few tasks that permitted conversation.

"I'm planning a new draft," Mistress Blair told her as they got to work. "Do you recall that Snail's Trail coverlet I made for the Grubers? I'm going to keep that lovely repeating curve but add small Rosepath blocks in between."

Elspeth slowly turned a wooden crank that wound the

threads onto the loom's back beam. "That does sound lovely." She hesitated, then said shyly, "I've been thinking through a new pattern in my head."

"You have?" Mistress Blair stood at the front of the loom, and her watchful gaze didn't stray from the warp threads sliding through her spread fingers, but she smiled with delight. "That pleases me!"

"I've no' had a chance to mark out the treadlings," Elspeth said quickly. "And I dinna ken if I can even do so—"

"Stop, there's a tangle . . . ah, I've got it. Elspeth, I'll help you draft your pattern. We'll work on it together, shall we?"

Elspeth felt her face flush with pleasure. "Oh, aye, I would like that!"

"I remember how I felt when I first wove a pattern of my own design." Mistress Blair smiled. "I remember when I wove my first yard of overshot at all. I felt like springtime inside." Her smile faded. "I would *never* have wished for my husband to lose his sight, but in truth I am much happier than I was before I took over the business. I love weaving out a new pattern. Had I not been forced to take charge, I would have spent the rest of my days as a—a shadow of the person I've become."

Elspeth thought of the joy and pride Mistress Blair took in her work. It must be hard for her to remember that if her husband had not suffered such misfortune, she would never have discovered her gift for fine weaving.

Mistress Blair blinked and shook off her momentary

sadness. "But you, Elspeth—you can start now! I've known many fine weavers who could follow a draft but could no more adapt a pattern to suit their own fancy than they could fly. A true weaver can't always be content to treadle someone else's designs."

"I dinna wish to take ye from your own work," Elspeth said anxiously.

Mistress Blair smiled. "Elspeth, knowing how you and Mercy whisper together, I suspect you already know I'm expecting a child. I can't imagine how I'll manage without your assistance. Teaching you about pattern drafting will help the business."

Once the warp was neatly wound around the loom's back beam, Elspeth spent the rest of the afternoon carefully passing the end of each thread through an eyehole made of string and attached to one of the harnesses, which was attached to a treadle. She followed Mistress Blair's new pattern draft, making sure that each thread would rise or fall properly when the treadles were stepped on. *One day I shall thread a design of my own making!* she thought. The notion made excitement bubble inside her.

All too soon, Elspeth saw shadows stretching across the floor. "I didna finish," she told Mistress Blair regretfully, "but I should soon be on my way."

Mercy overheard and frowned. "Can't you stay for evening meal?"

Elspeth shook her head. "I canna stay tonight, but I'll

be back tomorrow. Oh—and Mistress Blair?" Elspeth tried to keep her voice easy. "I need to visit MacLeod's apothecary. Are ye needing any dyestuffs? I could fetch something for ye, save ye a trip."

"Why, yes. I need logwood. Tell Dr. MacLeod to put it on my account." Mistress Blair held out a piece of woven cloth. "Here, take this with you. It's a gift for your grannie."

Elspeth recognized the bold pattern as one of Mistress Blair's originals, the one she called Pine Bough. "Oh, 'tis lovely!" she cried. "But I thought ye'd be sewing the panels together for a coverlet." Usually three long pieces of overshot cloth, each as wide as the loom permitted, were sewn together to make a bed-sized blanket.

"Not this time," Mistress Blair said lightly. "I was so pleased with how the new pattern wove out that I had Mercy cut the lengths into pieces and hem them as towels. I thought to give them to some of my special friends."

Elspeth felt as warmed by the gift as if Mistress Blair had presented her with a full coverlet. *I am a fortunate lass,* she thought as she turned toward the village.

Most of the merchants in Cross Creek sold a variety of goods, but Murdock MacLeod, a surgeon, specialized in medicines and such. He also carried logwood and cochineal, which Mistress Blair used to dye wool blue and red. A bell tinkled when Elspeth stepped into the small apothecary shop, which smelled of lavender and chalk and something sharp that she couldn't identify.

The room was empty. The door leading to the back room where Dr. MacLeod pulled teeth and set broken bones was ajar, however, and Elspeth heard several urgent male voices. "Wait," someone said, and then Dr. MacLeod appeared in the doorway. *Some of those Highlanders in Cross Creek, the merchants and such, they're not like us,* Duncan had said, and Elspeth was reminded of that as she looked at the physician's fine ruffled shirt, waistcoat with fancy trim, and matching frock coat with silver buttons. She saw no pine sprig stuck in a buttonhole. He held a piece of paper in his hand.

"It's just a girl," he muttered over his shoulder, then said to Elspeth, "Yes? Are you ill, or needing some medicine?" Dr. MacLeod's voice still carried a bit of Scottish burr.

"No, sir. I'm here for Mistress Blair. She did ask if ye'd be so kind as to send me off with a bit of logwood, and mark it against her account." Elspeth was grateful that Mistress Blair had given her good cause to come.

"Ah, yes. You're the weaver's girl. I remember now." He put the paper down on the counter and began scanning his shelves, which were crowded with vials and jars holding a bewildering variety of powders, pills, crushed leaves, seeds, dried flowers, shriveled roots, pieces of bark, and liquids of various colors.

Elspeth took a step sideways, trying to get a better look at the paper. It looked like a handbill, one of the small notices printed to advertise goods or call a meeting.

She'd seen such things nailed up about Cross Creek. Was this something to do with the Patriot cause?

The physician found the logwood and scooped some of the dark heartwood shavings onto a scale. Elspeth took another step closer to the handbill. It was illustrated with a snake and a pine tree. Where had she seen that before? Ah, yes—on the Patriot handbill Robbie had brought to the Gunns' *céilidh*. If only she knew how to read!

"Here you are." The physician poured the shavings onto a slip of brown paper, twisted it closed, and handed it to her.

"Yes, sir. Thank you." Elspeth hesitated. This man was likely a Patriot—and possibly working with Tall Tam Mac-Racken! But how to find out? "Pardon, sir, but is there any news of the rebellion today? My family lives a ways from town, and we're always hungry for news."

"There's none that I've heard."

Elspeth sighed, defeated. She'd learned nothing! Back on the street, she hooded the top of her *arisaid* over her head, considering. She needed bolder action.

Perhaps she should go inside the Patriots' tavern instead of just walking past. The thought made her shudder. What would Grannie or her cousins say to see Elspeth going alone into a tavern? But she wanted badly to catch Tall Tam MacRacken at the Black Bull. Then she'd truly have a tale to tell Grandda!

Scooping up her courage, Elspeth marched to the tavern. A man emerged as she approached, and laughter spilled onto the street. Elspeth sucked in her breath and stepped inside.

The room was smoky and smelled of ale and meat pies. Elspeth scanned the crowded room quickly. Several men wearing the sturdy breeches and shirts of farmers sat around one table, and a travel-stained family was eating dinner at another. A larger group of men clustered near the back. Some sat; some lounged against the wall. Some wore trim waistcoats; others wore work-worn breeches and homespun shirts. A woman in a grease-stained dress eeled among them with a jug of ale, refilling tankards.

A stout man gestured angrily with a long clay pipe. "It's more taxation without representation, that's what it is."

"We must take action!" another man insisted. "I'm ready to ride tonight."

They're all Patriots! Elspeth thought, and sudden fear made her skin clammy. What if the men who had confronted her and Grandda were here, and recognized her? Or what if Tall Tam were here? She scanned the group quickly—and saw someone else altogether.

Elspeth gasped and leaned against the door frame, a hand pressed to her mouth. At the edge of the Patriot group, two men sat at a small round table, holding pewter mugs and listening intently. One man was a stranger. Elspeth's gaze had locked on to the second man.

It was Mercy's father.

CHAPTER 7
SHATTERED

Aman who smelled of onions stepped on her foot as he came inside the tavern, and Elspeth bolted.

Robbie was waiting at Clear Spring, musket in hand. With his silent, reassuring presence beside her, Elspeth was scarcely aware of the forest's shadows as they started for home. Her mind was tumbling. Was Mr. Blair a Patriot? It suddenly seemed so. But . . . perhaps not. Perhaps he had sympathy with the Patriot cause—it might go no further than that.

Still, she couldn't avoid one horrifying realization. All along, she and her family had assumed that one of their fellow Scots was betraying them to the Patriots. But Mr. Blair knew almost as much about Elspeth as anyone.

He certainly knew when she was likely to be heading home for the day. And Elspeth had spoken of her cousins' Petersburg trip to Mercy, who might have mentioned it to her parents. *No, wait! It can't be Mr. Blair!* Elspeth thought with a flush of relief. The first time Patriots had threatened her family, Mercy had been with them. Mr. Blair surely wouldn't have sent Patriots out on a night when his own daughter was traveling with Grandda.

Elspeth didn't notice when Robbie stopped walking until he put a hand on her arm. "What is it?" she asked, instantly alert.

"Wheesht," he said softly. Elspeth's heart began to pound as they stood in darkness, listening to the night. A faint breeze sighed among the pine boughs far above them.

"There's no one about," Robbie said after a moment. "I didn't mean to put a fright in you, but I needed to be sure. I want to show you something."

Elspeth took a deep breath. "Where are we?"

"Less than a mile from your place." Robbie lifted the lantern. They stood beside a large forked branch that wind or lightning had tossed against an enormous pine. "Mark this spot well in your mind."

He led her away from the hunting trail. The open pine forest gave way to lower, swampier ground near the creek. When they came to a tangle of briers and grapevine, Robbie dropped to his knees and elbowed aside the dense veil. "I found this spot by accident once when I was tracking a deer and got caught in a storm. There's space enough to curl up beneath this log."

"Why are you showing me this?" Elspeth whispered.

"It's a safe place. A hiding place, should you ever

need it. You must be able to find it even in the dark."

No! Elspeth wanted to cry. She didn't want to know about hiding places, or the reasons she might need them. Just as she didn't want to know that Jennet's father had been watching her cabin, or that Mercy's father visited the Black Bull. Shivering, she snugged her mother's *arisaid* about her throat. *Let it keep you safe,* Grannie had said. Elspeth clutched the wool tightly. She needed some of her mother's courage.

Then she took a deep breath, straightened her shoulders, and took a long, careful look.

"I see," she told Robbie quietly. "I'll mind it well."

❦

Elspeth worried about facing Mr. Blair, afraid her suspicions would show. But for the next several days, he left for the village before she arrived.

In the third week of January, when a storm brought several inches of snow, Mercy's mother suggested that Elspeth spend two nights a week at the Blair home. "It seems harsh for you to travel back and forth in this weather," she fretted, while Mercy almost danced with delight behind her.

"I'll ask Grannie," Elspeth said cautiously, remembering how Grannie had scolded the last time Elspeth had asked to sleep over at the Blairs' home.

Duncan met her at Clear Spring that evening. He wore his great belted plaid, as he often did these days, and a few snowflakes dusted the thick wool. "Elspeth, me lass," he crowed, draping an arm over her shoulders as they set out toward home. "'Tis a fine evening!"

Elspeth couldn't help smiling. "And why is that? Your knees are almost blue with cold, and we've naught but a long walk ahead of us."

Duncan lowered his voice and switched to Gaelic. "I've news, that's why. You know the royal governor has been in exile on a ship off the coast. Well, he and some Loyalist leaders are ready to retake the colony."

"Are they, now?" Elspeth asked slowly.

"They want to raise an army of ten thousand men. General MacDonald is to assemble the Loyalists at Cross Creek on February twelfth. That Loyalist militia will march down the Cape Fear River toward Wilmington and rendezvous with British troops at the coast. The governor has already received assurances that British troops will come to his aid! Together, the soldiers and militia can seize control of North Carolina Colony—take it back from the Patriots."

Elspeth listened with a sinking heart. "What does this news mean for us? Grandda wants to sit clear of it all—"

"Surely he can't! Not now!" Duncan kicked through the snow with long, determined strides.

Elspeth caught at his plaid. "Duncan, don't stir the arguments back up! He won't change his mind."

"Well, I've a mind of my own."

"*Duncan!*" Elspeth stopped walking.

Her cousin turned. "Ah, now, don't fret. I can but try."

When they arrived at Elspeth's cabin, Duncan shared his news over a plate of black pudding. Grandda listened without comment, and Elspeth thought for a moment she saw something wistful in his eye. Then his face closed, and the look was gone. "This means nothing to us," he said. "And where did you come by this news, I wonder?"

"I stopped for a drink in Cross Creek, and—"

"I sent you to fetch your cousin home, not bide your time at a tavern."

Then came the argument Elspeth had dreaded. Before it was done, Grandda and Duncan were both shouting. Grannie sat silent with a harsh look in her eyes, and Elspeth wished mightily that she were back at the Blair house.

"You will mind me on this!" Grandda bellowed just before Duncan slammed out of the house. A moment later, Grandda plunged outside, too—whether to go after Duncan or simply work off his steam at the woodpile, Elspeth didn't know.

Elspeth scraped the rest of Grandda's meal back into the pot. "Grannie," she dared, "Mistress Blair suggested that I stay over at their house now and again while the weather is harsh."

Grannie waved her left hand. "Yes, yes. That's fine." She was staring at the door.

Elspeth blew out a breath. The men's argument still hung heavy and brittle in the air, but at least her own business was done.

Elspeth thought about her family's tangles as she lay in bed that night, sorting through the stray threads of information she had: Patriots taking special interest in them, some kind of bad blood with the MacRackens, Mr. Blair visiting the Black Bull. No matter how she tried to weave them together, she couldn't come up with whole cloth.

Well, perhaps she could learn something about the Patriots by spending more time with the Blairs. Elspeth rolled onto her side, curling up against drafts sneaking into the loft, as she considered. She needed to learn more about the MacRacken family, too. She should have accepted Jennet's invitation to visit.

As she remembered the look on Tall Tam's face when he stared at her in church, and the silent watch he'd held by her cabin, the thought of visiting Jennet's home made her muscles clench. But she'd never sort things out if she didn't find out what trouble stood between the two families. *I must talk with Jennet,* she thought, and with that resolve, she finally drifted to sleep.

That night Elspeth dreamed she was sitting at the loom, watching a beautiful pattern of her own design grow before her, thread by thread. She felt an immense satisfaction as she heard the beater bar hit home after every pass of her shuttle. Then the rhythmic thud shifted into a faster pounding. Only when Grandda shouted something below did the dream fade to groggy wakefulness.

Elspeth crawled to the loft edge and peered over. Grandda stood in his nightshirt before the latched door. The faint light of first dawn creeping through the window gleamed on the pistol in his hand. "Who's there, I say?" he shouted in Gaelic and again in English. "Speak up, or by God I'll—" He broke off suddenly, shot back the latch, and opened the door. Aunt Mary stumbled inside.

"Speak up, woman!" Grandda snapped in Gaelic. "What's brought you from your bed?"

"It's the boys," she cried. "My boys. They're gone."

Grandda was away after Robbie and Duncan for three days. Aunt Mary returned to her own cabin, afraid to leave again lest her sons come home or send word. Elspeth, waiting with Grannie, felt almost as alone as Mary. Grannie spent much of that time in bed, as if the news about Robbie and Duncan was more than she could face. Those cold, gray January days were longer than any Elspeth could remember.

The sun had set on the third day when the cabin door opened and Grandda walked inside. His mouth was set in a hard line and dark shadows ringed his eyes. "I found the boys," he announced, "and sent them home to their mother."

The soup simmering on the hearth boiled over and hissed into the fire. Elspeth reached blindly for a spoon to stir it down.

Grannie's eyes narrowed. "There's more."

"There's more." He shrugged out of his coat and sat down at the table across from his wife. "The deed was done before I caught up with them. They've signed on with the Loyalist militia."

Elspeth drew a deep breath. *Mo chreach.* Her cousins had chosen.

"Yet the boys are home?" Grannie asked, her tone hard.

"Just until the muster. The officers are still raising troops." Grandda ran a hand over his hair. "Elspeth, fetch me something to eat."

Elspeth quickly ladled a bowl of soup, put it on the table before him, and found some bread to go with it. When he gestured toward the whisky jug, she fetched that, too. All the while she felt her grandmother's anger crackling in the air.

Grannie let her husband finish his meal before she spoke again. "There's still more."

"Aye." He met her gaze. "When the boys get called, I'll be going with them."

A wordless cry of rage escaped from his wife. Shoving to her feet, she began to pace the little cabin, her eyes glittering like coals. Elspeth shrank down on a stool. Her mouth was as dry as cotton.

Grandda laid his forearms on the table. "I had no choice but to sign on, Morag. Duncan and Robbie know nothing of war. I can let them march off in ignorance, or I can go keep an eye on the young fools—"

Grannie snatched the calico bottle from the mantel and threw it against the wall. It shattered with a terrible crash and tinkling of glass. Elspeth nearly jumped from her skin.

"*Morag!*" Grandda looked grim. "It's not like last time—"

"And what do you know of what happened to me the last time you marched off to war?" Grannie stormed to the door and grabbed the old *arisaid* from its peg. "I'm going to see my grandsons. I won't be back before light. And don't *dare* come after me, Angus MacKinnon!" The door slammed behind her.

Elspeth grabbed the lantern and lit it quickly by the hearth. When she ran outside, she found her grandmother still struggling to wrap the long length of wool around her. "Grannie. Grannie! Here—take this. You'll get lost in the dark, else." Wordlessly Grannie accepted the lantern and stood rigid while Elspeth fastened the *arisaid* around her. Then she marched away. Elspeth watched the spot of light fade into the forest and struggled to hold back her tears.

Grandda appeared in the doorway. "Let her go, lass. She'll come back when she cools down."

"What's going to happen?" Elspeth asked, following him inside. She felt hollow.

"I don't know." He still spoke in Gaelic, which was as scary as anything else.

Elspeth sank to the floor and began picking up pieces of broken glass. An ache grew beneath her ribs. The precious calico bottle! Saved from the burning cottage by her mother, and carefully carried all the way from Scotland thirty years later. Shattered now.

Grandda sat down, planting elbows on knees. "Listen to me, *Elisaid*. Your grannie is angry with me. But mostly she's just afraid. Do you understand that? Last time I left her—well, you've heard the stories."

Elspeth nodded, staring at the shards of glass.

"I didn't bring my family all this way to fight in a war that's not of our doing." Grandda sighed. "Yet I can't blame the boys for what they did. I'd have done the same at their age."

Elspeth picked up a piece of glass, trying to picture Grandda as a young man. She imagined a mix of Duncan's high spirits and Robbie's good sense.

"I couldn't send the boys off to war on their own. I know what battle is. I can watch out for them, Elspeth. Do you understand?"

"I do." Elspeth understood more than she wanted to. Only Grandda knew what battle was. But only Grannie knew what it meant to be left behind. How could the two ever find common ground?

And where did all this leave *her*? With Grannie likely

having bad spells, and Aunt Mary almost as fragile? With Grandda and the boys gone to war, and Tall Tam MacRacken—or *someone*—angry that they hadn't joined forces with the Patriots? What if the Patriots swooped down upon the women and children, just as the British soldiers had back in Scotland?

"You're a strong girl, Elspeth—"

"No, I'm not!" she flared. "I'm not brave like my mother was. Nor like Grannie, either. I don't want this! What if you and the boys are gone come spring planting? Who will get the crops in? Who will make sure the land-lord gets his rent?"

"We'll find a way. We've got good neighbors; you'll not be all on your own. And the Loyalist men have been promised fair pay for their service."

I don't want fair pay and good neighbors! Elspeth wanted to shriek. She wanted what few shreds of her family remained to finally be safe and left alone. But it was too late for wishes. The Loyalist muster was only two weeks away.

Finally she looked up. "I'll try, Grandda. I'll do my best to take care of Grannie while you're gone."

"You'll do right fine, child." He rested one callused hand on her head. "Right fine."

CHAPTER 8
JENNET'S TALE

Most of Grandda's friends were delighted to learn that he'd enlisted with the Loyalist militia. *Captain MacKinnon*, they called him, and within a few days, nineteen men had volunteered to march off with him. "I didna mean for it to be so," Grandda muttered, but he went to Cross Creek to meet with the Loyalist officers. He came home with bad news.

"They're asking for the captains to stay with the banner in the village," he said, eyeing Grannie warily. "Men from the backcountry are coming in to volunteer. I'll need to leave in the morning."

At dawn, while Grandda was doing chores, Grannie left for Aunt Mary's. *Forgive him—just a little!* Elspeth begged silently. *At least say good-bye!* But Grannie left without a word.

After Elspeth made breakfast, Grandda dressed

carefully in his little-wrap—a short length of tartan cloth worn around the waist, with a shirt, waistcoat, and jacket above. He retrieved his old broadsword from over the mantel. "I didna expect to carry this again," he murmured, testing the heft in his hand. Then he crouched by the trunk they'd brought from Scotland, rummaged inside, and paused with the old hat in his hand. "I thought to wear this today, for luck," he said thoughtfully, fingering the limp white ribbon rose. "But I dinna think so now. Last time I marched to war, 'twas *against* the king of England, not for him."

He placed the cap carefully back into the trunk before retrieving something else. "Here, lass." When Elspeth held out her hand, Grandda placed in her palm a tiny piece of tartan fabric woven in red, black, and green. He regarded the frayed, dirty scrap with a look of reverence. "I carried that all the time I was in hiding and in prison. 'Twas foolish, perhaps, because the law forbade the tartan. I would have been punished sore hard had the soldiers found it. But I kept it so I'd always ken I was a Scot."

As if we could ever forget that! Elspeth thought. Being Scottish was a weight they hauled behind them through life.

"I canna leave home without this, I think. Your grannie gave it to me." He tucked the scrap of cloth into his pocket, then considered his granddaughter. "I ken well enough why she didna wish to say good-bye. But

I'll be in Cross Creek for several days yet, aye? We're still gatherin' in the boys. See if she'll come in to town with you before we march off."

Elspeth knocked and eased open the Blairs' front door. "Elspeth!" Mercy cried, dropping her shuttle. "All this time and no sign of you! Were you sick?"

"Grannie had a wee bad spell," Elspeth said, fanning cold fingers toward the fire. She had decided not to speak too freely about what had happened.

"Is she well now?" Mistress Blair looked concerned.

"Well enough. 'Tis kind of ye to ask. I'll get on to work, aye?"

Elspeth settled at her loom, avoiding her friend's troubled gaze. She had considered asking Mercy about her father's loyalties but decided against it. Mr. Blair sat in his usual spot, picking bits of dirt from a raw fleece, and Elspeth eyed him warily over the beater bar. What would he say if he knew the MacKinnon men had pledged to fight with the Loyalists? Would it matter?

This trouble has chased me even here, she thought, and that seemed almost worst of all.

The next day, Mistress Blair finished hemming a new wool blanket. "Elspeth," she said, "this is intended for Mistress MacAlister. Do you know her?"

"If ye mean Mistress Lovedy MacAlister, I do, aye. She lives along Panther Creek."

Mistress Blair rubbed her back as if it ached. The baby she carried was just starting to show beneath her apron. "Would you deliver the blanket for me? I believe Mistress MacAlister speaks only Gaelic. She brought someone who knew a bit of English when she made the order."

"Aye, I can do that," Elspeth said slowly. Jennet Mac-Racken lived along Panther Creek. *If I hurry,* she thought, *I can visit Jennet after.*

Elspeth delivered the blanket to a delighted Mistress MacAlister, then asked directions to the MacRacken mill. It was only half a mile or so farther. The huge mill wheel was still and silent, but a thin plume of smoke danced from the chimney of the small frame house nearby.

Elspeth paused on the outskirts of the clearing, nerves fluttering. Taking a deep breath, she pulled the *arisaid* firmly around her shoulders. Her mother wouldn't have been afraid.

As Elspeth approached the house, she called a greeting in Gaelic. No one appeared. Before her courage deserted her, Elspeth knocked on the door. A moment later it cracked open, and Jennet peered out. A surprised smile lit her face. *"Elisaid!"* The door opened wide. *"Ciamar a tha thu?"*

"I am well," Elspeth answered. She stepped inside the MacRacken home, fighting down another spurt of unease as the door shut behind her. But the house didn't look menacing. Aside from having walls of sawn boards instead of logs, it didn't look much different from her own. The lower room boasted two beds, a table and benches, a hutch for dishes, and several trunks. A ladder led to the loft.

"Will you bide awhile?" Jennet asked. "I should finish those." She gestured toward a round, flat griddle balanced over the fire. She was baking hoecakes.

Elspeth settled gingerly onto a bench. "I can't stay but a minute. Is . . . is your father home?" She couldn't help asking.

Jennet crouched by the griddle. "No, he and my uncle are out this afternoon. They found a crack in the water-wheel's rim and went to see the blacksmith. That's why I didn't answer right away." Her face reddened. "I get nervous when I'm alone. I'm not used to this dark place yet."

"Nor am I," Elspeth admitted. "And . . . and all the trouble—this war—it doesn't help."

"No." Jennet used a fork to carefully turn a hoecake on the griddle. "We thought the only fighting would be in the northern colonies."

"Now it seems there may be fighting right here in North Carolina Colony." Elspeth tried to keep her voice casual. "Do you think your father will join in? Become a Patriot or a Loyalist?"

"I don't know."

Jings. That wasn't very helpful. Elspeth tried a new approach. "I think these troubles are hardest on people my grandparents' age, because of what happened back in Scotland. The '45."

Jennet eased a golden-brown hoecake from the griddle to a platter. "I suppose so. None of my grandparents are still alive. I've just my father and my uncle."

Elspeth's palms were beginning to feel damp. She wasn't getting *anywhere*. Suppose Tall Tam MacRacken found her inside his home, questioning Jennet about the past? But she couldn't give up—not quite yet. "Where did you live in Scotland?" she asked, trying to keep her voice light. "We're from the Isle of Skye. Have you ever been there?"

"No. We lived away from the sea." Jennet patted a handful of the cornmeal mixture into a flat round and placed it on the griddle.

If Jennet knew anything about the bad blood between the two families, she was hiding it well. More likely, Jennet didn't know anything about it.

"Here." Jennet held the platter up to Elspeth. "Please, have one. I wish we had more to offer."

"This is fine, thank you." Elspeth nibbled one of the hot cakes. Jennet's hospitality made her feel worse.

Jennet took a cake to munch also, still keeping an eye on her griddle. "If you're from Skye, did you eat sea tangle? My mother's mother once lived near the sea, and I recall her telling how she loved to eat stalks of sea tangle raw."

Elspeth's heart suddenly raced. Jennet's grandmother had once lived near the sea! Had she once lived on Skye and known Grannie? All this time, Elspeth had assumed that Grannie had been wronged by a MacRacken. But, of course, the bad blood could be between Grannie and someone from Jennet's *mother's* side, too.

"Or sometimes they roasted sea tangle over peat embers," Jennet chattered on, "and ate it with bannocks. Is that how you had it?"

"It is," Elspeth murmured. She'd never cared overmuch for the seaweed known as sea tangle, but suddenly a flood of homesickness almost took her breath away. She missed tasting sea tangle, smelling salt breezes, hearing seagulls' cries. Most of all, she missed the open sky.

"*Elisaid?*" Jennet asked anxiously. "Are you well?"

"Just—just homesick. I miss the sea." Avoiding Jennet's gaze, Elspeth got to her feet and studied the objects on the MacRackens' mantel. "Did these things come from Scotland?" She touched a small silver jug. The rim had been hammered into a pretty scalloped design; the handle had a graceful flair. And a fancy curved line had been marked into the center of the jug.

"Isn't it pretty?" Jennet said proudly, coming to stand beside Elspeth. "It belonged to my mother. See?" She pointed at the curved line. "Do you know your letters?"

Elspeth shook her head.

"I just know this one," Jennet said. "It's a *C*. My mother was a Campbell, and that's their letter."

A *C*, for Campbell. *Campbell.* Why did that sound

familiar? Elspeth felt something tug at her memory, but try as she might, she couldn't grab it.

Well, she'd accomplished what she could. "I must be on my way," she told Jennet. "I work for a weaver in Cross Creek, and she's expecting me back."

"Please come again, if you're passing," Jennet said eagerly. "Or anytime."

Elspeth was glad to leave the MacRacken house behind. As she hurried back toward Cross Creek, she tried to piece together a possible story from the new scraps of information. Jennet's mother's mother had once lived on Skye. Many years ago she, or someone in her family, must have done Grannie some wrong so terrible that the grudge was nursed even now.

"But how am I supposed to know what," Elspeth muttered, "when Grannie won't say, and Aunt Mary won't say, and no one else seems to know?" *Campbell.* Jennet's mother had been a Campbell. If only—

"Oh!" Elspeth spoke so sharply that a white-faced black squirrel, wrestling with a huge, prickly pinecone among the thick carpet of fallen needles, darted away. Elspeth stood still as a pine, her breath coming in puffs of hoary white, as she tried to remember. She had asked Grandda if he'd known any MacRackens who'd fought against Prince Charlie during The '45, and he'd said no: *No, lass, not that I can say. 'Twas the Campbells and their ilk, mostly.*

That must be it! Elspeth's Grannie had been on one side of the war in Scotland, Jennet's grandmother on the other. And she, or one of those Campbells, had done Grannie some terrible wrong.

Was that wrong being repeated here in North Carolina? Elspeth's grandfather and cousins had joined the Loyalists, fighting for the British. Had Jennet's father chosen for the Patriots? And might he yet be planning some terrible new strike against Elspeth's family?

When Elspeth left the Blair home that afternoon, Robbie was waiting beneath the trees across the lane. She hurried to meet him. "What are you doing here? Is something wrong?"

"I thought to walk you home."

The day was cloudy and cold. A woodpecker's sharp cry rang through the woods. "Thank you," Elspeth said, grateful for the company. She hadn't expected it, now that her cousins had enlisted.

"And I wanted to talk to you. Elspeth, I'm sorry about what's happened. When Duncan and Grandda and me are away, you'll be the one left behind."

"Well . . . and Grannie, and your mother."

"If trouble comes, I'm afraid you're the only one who might keep her wits about her." Robbie didn't meet her eye. Despite his long, easy stride, he was constantly surveying their surroundings for any sign of trouble.

"I didn't think it would come to this."

Elspeth didn't know what to say.

"It was Duncan." Robbie sighed. "You know how he can be. He acts before he thinks. He was hot to sign on with the Loyalists. I didn't want to sign up without Grandda's approval, but when I heard Duncan slipping out that night, I went after him. He wouldn't come home, so I enlisted, too—to keep an eye on him, aye? But I never thought Grandda would sign on because of us."

"Well, it's done now." Elspeth was proud of the even tone in her voice. Then she remembered her visit with Jennet. "Robbie, did Tall Tam MacRacken sign on with Grandda?"

"He did not."

I'm not surprised by that, Elspeth thought.

"Nor did Red John MacKay, or Neill MacNeill," Robbie added. "Some still want no part in this fight. And I'll judge no man for that."

They walked in a brooding silence. Should she tell Robbie about Tall Tam watching the cabin, and what she'd learned about Jennet's grandmother? Was there anything to be gained by adding to his burden of worry? Elspeth was still considering as they rounded the final bend to her cabin. Perhaps—

Robbie jerked to a stop with an oath. "*Beul sìos oirbh!*"

A body was hanging from a tree ahead, twisting limply in the light breeze.

"*Stay here*," Robbie ordered fiercely, and then he began to run. Elspeth's knees went wobbly, and she thought she might be sick. Still, she needed to see. She stumbled after her cousin with a sob catching in her throat.

In the gray light, she was upon the figure before she realized that someone had fashioned a man's body from straw and cloth. The figure was dressed in a dirty linen shirt and breeches, but a length of tartan plaid was wrapped around it. The stuffed cloth head flopped limply to one side over the rope looped around the neck.

Robbie cursed again as he snatched his knife and slashed the rope. The straw man flopped to the ground. Elspeth pressed one hand against her belly. Eyes closed, she sucked in slow breaths of cold, damp air.

Only then was she able to take a closer look. She didn't recognize the tattered tartan cloth. But a closer inspection showed that the linen shirt was not merely dirty. A series of letters had been marked upon it with what looked like tar.

"Does that say something?" Elspeth asked, pointing. She couldn't bring herself to touch the horrid thing.

Robbie stood with fists clenched. "'MacKinnon'," he said finally. "It says 'MacKinnon'."

CHAPTER 9
THE MUSTER

The next week passed without incident, although Elspeth dreaded her cousins' departure. To her surprise, when muster day came, Grannie accompanied her and Aunt Mary to Cross Creek to see their men off.

The Loyalist militia camped on the outskirts of the village was a resplendent lot. Almost all of the men were Highlanders—a few from plantations along the Cape Fear River, many more from rude cabins deep in the woods. Like Grandda, most wore the little-wrap of tartan cloth belted around their waists, with a shirt and coat above. Some wore English breeches. A few wore the great plaid wrapped round their waists and pulled up over their shoulders. Their stockings were tartan, too, held up by strips of cloth tied just below the knee.

When the men drilled, their breaths clouded in the cold air. The British flag snapped in the wind. Alasdair MacKay and two other pipers provided martial music. Watching

Grandda, Elspeth realized how difficult it must have been for him to counsel patience. He strode across the field with the vigor of a young man, and his voice rang with authority. When he demonstrated use of the broadsword to a group of young men, his eyes glinted with an old fire. "Aye, laddie, that's the way," he called. "Grip firm with both hands afore ye swing."

The field was ringed with spectators—mothers, sweethearts, and others come just to watch. Elspeth scanned the throng and saw Baker Pigeon standing in a clump of men, silently observing. Had *they* left the straw figure hanging in the tree? Were Patriot spies here, collecting information? Once she thought she glimpsed Tall Tam MacRacken across the field, but she couldn't be sure.

The MacKinnon men came to greet the women when dismissed from drill, Duncan bounding ahead. "Are we not a sight to behold?" he asked. "Don't look so low, Mother! We'll be at Wilmington soon enough, and we'll meet British troops there. Then we'll claim the southern colonies for the king. And on the other end of a few weeks' service are two hundred acres of land!"

"War generally involves more than marching and claiming," Grannie observed tartly as Grandda and Robbie joined them.

"It can," Grandda acknowledged, then added, "I'm glad you came, Morag."

"How many have mustered?" Grannie asked. "I heard

that the officers, MacDonald and MacLeod, promised the governor a force of three thousand Highlanders."

Grandda looked over the field. "We've about half that."

"Less than seven hundred guns," Robbie added quietly. "And no more than eighty broadswords."

"So few." Grannie sounded bleak. "Heaven help you."

Duncan shrugged and pushed long black curls from his face. "We'll pick up more guns along the way. We've got sanction to claim weapons for the king's cause."

All too soon, drums began to rattle. "We need to get back," Grandda said. Grannie nodded, pursing her lips. Aunt Mary handed the men packets of dried fruit to tuck into their *sporans*—the pouches they wore at their waists.

Elspeth clung to Grandda and each of her cousins in turn. They smelled of wool and wood smoke and sweat, and she couldn't get enough. Grandda gave her shoulder an extra squeeze. Robbie looked her in the eye and nodded, as if to say, *It will be hard, but I know you can manage.* Duncan swung her from the ground as if they were dancing, round and round until her vision blurred. By the time she planted her feet and caught her breath, he was gone.

The militiamen formed a thick, colorful column. The bagpipes' shrill wails rose above the drums' rattle. Someone shouted an order, and the men began to march. Elspeth felt a lump rise in her throat. She waved her handkerchief as her men passed, but could find no voice to cheer. Aunt Mary wept silently. Grannie stood like a stone.

When the column had finally disappeared down the Wilmington Road, the crowds began to drift away. Grannie didn't move and Elspeth waited, afraid to disturb her thoughts. But suddenly the fine hairs on the back of Elspeth's neck prickled. Slowly she turned her head.

Tall Tam MacRacken stood not ten paces behind them. Staring.

Elspeth could bear no more. She marched toward Jennet's father, demanding "What do you want?" Instead of answering, he turned and disappeared into the crowd.

He'll not show his hand here—amongst people, in broad sun, Elspeth thought. His kind moved at night. Left terrifying warnings hanging from trees.

She looked back at the empty road, at her grandmother and aunt still staring mutely toward Wilmington, and took a deep breath. She had never felt so alone.

Grannie told Elspeth to spend the night in Cross Creek. "I'll stay with Mary," Grannie said.

Together they walked to the Blair home, where Elspeth showed them the overshot coverlet panel growing on her loom. Grannie and Aunt Mary lingered over the fabric appreciatively, and Elspeth flushed with pride. "Tell Mistress Blair I am grateful for all she is teaching you," Grannie said to Elspeth in Gaelic. When Elspeth interpreted, the weaver smiled and nodded. "'Tis my pleasure to have such a hard and willing worker. Please tell her so."

Elspeth chewed her lower lip as she watched Grannie and Aunt Mary start for home. What if Tall Tam was waiting for them on the path? What if he and the Patriots had another surprise waiting?

"We shall work today on that original pattern you told me about," Mistress Blair announced. She spread out samples she'd woven over the years: Rosepath, Snowball, Snail's Trail, Chariot Wheel, her own Pine Bough pattern. She helped Elspeth identify the treadling sequence that created each design. Then they began ordering the design Elspeth had envisioned, marking out the treadlings on a scrap of paper. Before Elspeth knew it, the light was fading and Mercy was home from Cross Creek with her father in tow.

"I thank ye for this," Elspeth said. She wished she knew enough words, in any language, to let Mistress Blair know how grateful she was—not just for this new opportunity, but for keeping her mind occupied. Mistress Blair squeezed her shoulder.

They all sat down to Mercy's nice supper of stewed chicken baked into a pastry crust. "So the Loyalist militia is gone," Mr. Blair said. "And your grandfather with them, Elspeth?"

Elspeth froze. It was no secret, surely—but still! "Aye," she said finally.

"I stepped outside when those bagpipes began." He felt carefully for his mug and took a long drink. "What a wild sound!"

Elspeth stared at her plate. Mr. Blair had never been anything but kind to her. Elspeth wished she could trust him, as she did his wife and daughter. But since learning that he kept company with Patriots at the Black Bull, she could not.

The next morning, Mr. Blair wound a dozen shuttle quills with yarn for his wife and Elspeth, and he carded a basket of wool—chores he could do by touch. After the midday meal, Mistress Blair asked if he wished to walk into the village. "I need to see Mistress Owens about her coverlet," she said. "The yarn she supplied is running short, and I'm feeling up to a walk today."

After they bundled up and left, Elspeth got up to fetch the quills. Each would fit neatly into one of her shuttles, and she wanted them within reach of her loom. As she walked to the table, something on the floor near the door caught her eye.

Elspeth scooped it up—a slip of paper, folded into a tight wad. One of Mercy's parents must have dropped it. She opened her mouth to tell Mercy, then closed it again. Unfolding the paper, she scanned a string of letters. They were unevenly written, and the ink was smeared in places.

Suppose this was a note about the war? It might prove, once and for all, where Mr. Blair's loyalties lay.

She glanced over her shoulder, but Mercy was washing dishes. Quickly Elspeth slipped the note into her pocket, fetched her quills, and went back to her loom. Her face was hot. She felt like a thief. She didn't even know how she could find out what was written on the note. Grandda could read English, and Robbie a bit as well, but they couldn't help her now.

Elspeth slid onto her loom bench. As she fit one of the quills into her shuttle, she found herself thinking about Mr. Blair. He had once been a master weaver and now could do nothing more than the tasks usually given to children. But he never complained. She stared at the shuttle, picturing him patiently winding the quills that morning...

Ah.

"Mercy, is your father cack-handed?" she asked.

Mercy stared, her dishrag dripping hot water onto the floor. "Is he *what?*"

Jings! How did the English say it? "Does he favor his left hand for tasks?"

"Not that I've noticed. Why is it you ask?"

"I—I was just thinking that he did us a kindly turn this morn, winding the quills."

Mercy shrugged and turned back to her dishes. "He likes having something to do. It's hard for a man to sit idle while his wife works."

Elspeth made a few passes with her shuttle, but her mind was racing. Had Mr. Blair favored his left hand while working? She wasn't certain. A cack-handed person would smear ink as he wrote, and a man almost blind would form crooked letters. Surely he, not Mistress Blair, had dropped the note.

Elspeth couldn't help hoping that she'd found something important. When she left the Blairs that afternoon, the note was in her pocket. Once at home, she climbed to the loft, rolled the note into a tiny tube, and slid it into her little wooden needle case. It would be safe there until someone she trusted could read it for her.

The days dragged by. Grannie spent much of her time sitting near the fire, staring at something far away. Elspeth now had barn chores and woodchopping to do, on top of helping with meals and cleaning. She went about the little farm with nerves quivering, always listening. The forest had never seemed so threatening. Aunt Mary sometimes came to stay, hunched and quiet, but most neighbors clung to their own clearings. At church on Sunday, Elspeth saw the few remaining men eyeing each other uneasily during prayers.

Every second day Elspeth escaped to the Blairs'. She was still terrified of seeing a Patriot loom from the forest gloom in front of her. But she wrapped herself in her mother's *arisaid* and, so armored, set forth.

One day, when her men had been gone for a little more than a week, Elspeth walked through Cross Creek after leaving the Blairs'. Even in the village, Elspeth sensed people waiting. Watching. Wondering. She smelled bread burning in a shop where a girl in a flour-speckled cap hung out the window, looking for news instead of tending the oven. She heard a mother snap at her young son, rounding on him because there was no one else to round on. When Elspeth circled near the print shop where broadsides were posted, hoping to hear some news, she heard two men shouting at each other. They might have come to blows if another man, a sturdy freight hauler, hadn't shrugged out of the wooden frame he used to pack cargo and separated the two.

I'm for home, Elspeth decided. Tempers were high, and there was no reason to linger. Grandda had said it would likely be two weeks or more before the Loyalist militia reached Wilmington, so it was too soon to hope for news of them.

She stepped into the street, then quickly jumped back as a horse pounded past, straddled by a boy riding as if chased by the devil. She frowned—no need to risk running down good folk! Then her attention was grabbed by a shout from down the street, where the boy had tumbled to the ground. *Gaelic.* Someone was yelling in Gaelic.

A finger of fear flicked at Elspeth's spine. She snatched up her skirt and ran. A crowd was quickly forming around the boy. His horse stood with head hung low, sides heaving.

Elspeth tried to elbow close, but a burly man pushed her aside. "What's the news?" he asked in English. Elspeth heard more snatches of Gaelic, hurried and harsh.

Then a woman in front of her began to wail. Elspeth grabbed her arm. "*Dé?*" she demanded. *What?* But the woman shook her head, unable to speak.

Elspeth shoved frantically toward the rider. He looked no older than she was. His face was tight with fatigue and . . . and something more. He wore breeches, but a band of tartan adorned his hat. "Tell it again," someone cried. Hands were raised for quiet.

"It's the Highland militia," the boy said in Gaelic. "The men didn't make it to Wilmington. They met a force of Patriot militia this dawn at the bridge over Widow Moore's creek."

Elspeth's heart began to thump painfully in her chest. "Where is that?" someone asked. "Let the boy tell it!" someone else snapped. Another man grabbed the rider's arm. "God's eyeballs, lad, what happened? Did the Loyalists take the day?"

"They did not," the boy said, his voice trembling. "It was a sore defeat. Most all of the Highlanders are captured or dead."

CHAPTER 10
CAPTURED OR DEAD

Captured or dead. Grandda. Robbie. Duncan. *Captured or dead.* Giving Grannie and Aunt Mary that news was the hardest thing Elspeth had ever done. Aunt Mary's face went white, and she dropped abruptly to a stool. The spoon Grannie held slipped to the floor. The clatter echoed like a gunshot.

"I'm sorry," Elspeth whispered. A dull ache had lodged beneath her ribcage. She thought suddenly of Mistress Blair, with her kind words and comforting tone, and wished she could have taken the news to her instead.

No one slept that night. Elspeth came down the ladder at first light and found her grandmother and aunt already stirring up the fire. "I'm going to see if anyone has news," Elspeth said.

"I'll come, too," Aunt Mary said. "But we shouldn't go to Cross Creek. Patriots will likely seize the village in force now."

Grannie considered. "Go to the church. Folks will gather there. But, *Elisaid,* if there's news, bring it to me here."

Elspeth nodded, her stomach full of ice. If the news brought grief, Grannie wanted to hear it in private.

"And I need you to haul water for me before you leave. I'm going to do laundry."

"Laundry?" Elspeth repeated. Laundry, now? That was a harsh task in this weather, and although Grannie could scrub and rinse with only one good hand, hanging clothes to dry was a challenge. Then Elspeth nodded. Grannie needed to keep busy—very, very busy. Elspeth and Aunt Mary hauled water, built a fire in the outside firepit, and left Grannie to her scrubbing.

Elspeth was grateful for even her aunt's silent company as they drove the cart to church, where a handful of anxious Scots huddled together for comfort. Neill MacNeill reported that Patriot militia had occupied Cross Creek, but no one knew more. They passed most of the day there, sometimes praying, sometimes singing psalms. And waiting. Waiting. Waiting.

Afternoon shadows were growing long when Red John MacKay, Alasdair the piper's father, brought the first scrap of real news. "I am come from Moores Creek," he announced grimly. "I talked to a friend who lives not three miles from the place. The defeat was as bad as they say. But my friend believes that some of the Loyalists managed to escape the field." He looked from face to face, as if wanting to give his desperate friends and neighbors a bit of hope. Elspeth clung to it. Please, God, let *her* men be among those who had escaped.

"But . . . where are they, then?" someone asked.

Red John spread his hands. "Hiding in the swamps and forest. The Patriots are beating the ground for them, you can be sure of that."

"It's just like Culloden," an old man muttered.

"There's more." Red John rubbed his eyes. "I cut through the woods coming home, and I saw two cabins burning on the way. I've no doubt the Patriots are punishing Loyalist families."

Elspeth clenched her fists until her fingernails dug into the skin. *So,* she thought, *it has begun.*

Aunt Mary touched her arm. "Come along, Elspeth. We must go home."

They left the comfort of church and friends and headed into the twilight. Neither spoke until they reached the fork that led to Aunt Mary's cabin. "Can you tend to your grandmother alone?" Aunt Mary asked, pulling Moll to a halt. "If Robbie and Duncan escaped the field, they'll head home."

"I can, but . . . Red John MacKay said the Patriots are searching for the soldiers. I don't think the boys will dare come home." Elspeth wanted to put four stout log walls between herself and the night. "I think you'd be safer staying with us, not all alone."

Aunt Mary shook her head. "I have nothing left in life but my sons. I'm going home to wait for them." She pressed the reins into Elspeth's hands and climbed down.

Elspeth found Grannie sitting by the hearth in the cabin, looking exhausted. She did no more than nod when Elspeth told her what they'd learned. Elspeth heated some soup for supper, then went outside to finish chores. She went along the line where the laundry had been draped, wringing and straightening. She could tell how agitated her grandmother had been, because almost every scrap of cloth they owned had been carried outside: extra clothes, dirty rags, the spare linen sheets, even the beautiful, never-used towel Mistress Blair had given them. After the laundry was tended, Elspeth emptied the heavy iron wash kettle and tipped it to guard against rust. She milked the cow and fed the animals. She hauled water and carried firewood inside and washed the dishes.

And still that night, though she ached with fatigue and tension, she couldn't sleep. Instead she listened. She heard the eaves creak in the wind, and an owl hooting. Much later, she heard Grannie get up to put a log on the fire.

Elspeth's thoughts clung to her grandfather and cousins. Did they yet live? If they *had* escaped the field, where were they? On the run? Hiding in some swamp, wet and cold and hungry? Despite what Aunt Mary had said, Elspeth didn't believe they'd risk coming home. Not with the Patriots looking for them. So where could they hide?

Suddenly she sat up. She didn't know where to look for Duncan or Grandda. But if *Robbie* had escaped . . .

She hadn't undressed before lying down, so she fumbled only for her shoes before creeping down the ladder. Grannie sat hunched on the stool by the hearth again. The firelight flickered on her face—one cheek wrinkled with age, the other smooth and shiny from the thirty-year-old scars.

She's been through too much, Elspeth thought. "You should lie down," she said softly.

Grannie blinked. "Peggy? Is that you? Dawn's not come. Why are you up?"

"I . . . I have an errand," Elspeth said. In the faint light, she wrapped several leftover hoecakes in cloth and put them in a basket, then added a bit of ham. If only Grannie hadn't broken the calico bottle! Well, nothing for it.

Grannie looked up again as Elspeth wrapped the *arisaid* around herself. "Where are you taking that food?" she asked sharply.

Elspeth hesitated.

"Oh!" Grannie suddenly put a finger over her lips. "It's for your da, isn't it? He's hiding in the heather. You go on, then. Don't let the soldiers see you."

Elspeth slipped outside. She stood still, willing her knees to stop trembling. The night air was cold and damp against her cheeks. She jerked in alarm at a sudden rustling sound, then realized it was no more than a shirt or blanket on the clothesline, flapping in the breeze. She took a deep breath, trying to slow her racing heart.

It took everything she had not to turn and bolt back inside the cabin. Elspeth had never ventured into the forest at night without a lantern clenched in one hand. But tonight she dared not carry a light—not when vengeful Patriot soldiers were about, searching for Loyalists.

After a few moments, Elspeth could make out the silhouette of the barn and see where the path she wanted led from the clearing. She clutched the wool *arisaid* in both hands, trying to draw her mother's courage from the fibers. Then she drew a deep breath and set out.

Beneath the towering pines, the half-moon's feeble light disappeared. At home, back on Skye, the moon was a better companion. Elspeth crept along the path, her eyes straining. Once, she strayed from the hard-packed trail, feeling instead the thick, spongy layer of pine needles underfoot. *I'm lost!* she thought, tasting panic bitter on her tongue. But after a moment she caught her wits and felt gingerly about with one foot until she found the trail again.

It took forever to reach the forked branch leaning against the huge pine that Robbie had shown her. Then she had to leave the path. Swallowing the fear that threatened to choke off her breathing, she concentrated on finding landmarks. She felt the ground grow moist beneath her feet and heard the creek dancing somewhere

ahead of her. The tangle of grapevines and briers should
be just ahead—

"*Elisaid?*"

The whisper sounded so close to her ear that Elspeth
bit her tongue to hold in a shriek. "Robbie?" she breathed,
her heart racing. A shadow separated from a tree trunk,
and then she disappeared into her cousin's fierce hug.
He smelled different now—mud and gunpowder and
blood mingled with sweat and wool. "I'm so glad you're
here," she whispered into his shoulder. "I've been so
frightened!"

"But you came. I *knew* you'd come. Come, sit down."

They eased to the damp ground and leaned against
a tree. "Are you hurt?" Elspeth asked.

"Just bruised." He drew a deep, shuddering breath.
"But Duncan . . . Duncan is dead."

His whisper was like a punch in the gut. The night
whirled and Elspeth struggled to breathe. "Are you sure?"

"He is dead," Robbie repeated grimly. "I saw it. I know."

I can't cry now, Elspeth thought. *I don't have time to cry
now.* But her body didn't listen, and for a long while she
wept silently on Robbie's shoulder. She wept for Duncan—
laughing, dancing Duncan—and for broken dreams and
old heartaches.

Finally she sat up, wiping her nose on her sleeve.
"What of Grandda?" she asked, bracing for another blow.

"I don't know. I didn't see. The men with broadswords

went ahead." And Robbie told Elspeth what had happened: how they'd come to realize that Patriots were stalking them; how they'd tried to avoid a battle, wanting only to reach the coast and join the promised British troops; of their nightmarish nighttime march through snake- and alligator-infested swamps, trying to reach the only bridge across Moores Creek—twenty miles above Wilmington—before the Patriots cut them off.

"But the Patriots were camped on the far side of the bridge. Our officers decided to attack. They didn't know how well entrenched the Patriots were, or that they had cannons." Robbie sounded dazed.

Elspeth recognized the haunted tone in his voice.

As he told his tale, she could picture the bridge spanning the rushing creek. The experienced fighters—Grandda among them—had led the charge. Bagpipes screamed, and the men bellowed Gaelic war cries and "For King George and broadswords!" They found that the Patriots had removed planks from the bridge and greased the remaining beams. Using their swords for balance, they tried to pick their way across the bridge. The rest of the Loyalist militia, including Robbie and Duncan, advanced behind them.

The Patriots, hidden in the brush atop a rise on the far side of the creek, had waited until the Loyalists were within thirty paces before raining musketry and cannon fire down upon them.

"I kept by Duncan," Robbie said. "I was afraid his boasts might prove bigger than he was. But he never paused, Elspeth. He lived up to it all at that bridge. He was fierce brave."

Elspeth nodded. She could see Duncan running at that bridge.

"It was over in minutes." Robbie shuddered again. "Most of the advance men were cut down—but I didn't see Grandda. Some men were killed outright. Some fell off the bridge and likely drowned. And then came fire behind us, too. The Patriots had snuck a force around, somehow. That's when the rest of us ran. We split up fast to make it harder on them hunting us."

"I knew you wouldn't dare go home," Elspeth said. "That's why I came here, and in the night."

Robbie squeezed her hand. "You did well. But you should go now, before daylight comes."

"What will happen now? What will you do?"

"I don't know. Stay hid and see what happens."

It is just like The '45, Elspeth thought bitterly. *Our men cut down or hiding, and their women left to face what comes.* The MacKinnons had chosen to fight for the British king this time, instead of against him—and *still* they had suffered defeat.

"I'll try to come again tonight," she said. "Here, I brought you some food."

"Good lass. I haven't eaten in two days." Robbie ate

quickly, then paused. "Elspeth . . . don't tell Mother or Grannie where I am, or about Duncan. It's too dangerous."

Elspeth nodded, feeling a bit more weight settle on her shoulders. "I'll see you tonight," she whispered. "Oh! Wait." She fished in her pocket, then pulled out the wooden needle case and pressed it into his hand. "There's a note inside. Read it when daylight comes, and tell me tonight what it says."

"What is this about?"

"Maybe nothing. I need to know what it says first." There was no time to tell the whole story. After another hard hug, they parted. Robbie melted back into his hiding place, and Elspeth began picking her way back uphill toward the hunting path.

The ache was burning beneath her ribs again. It hurt to breathe. Duncan. They'd lost Duncan.

But tonight, she would find out if the note Mr. Blair had dropped was a shopping list or a message to the Patriots. "And pray God I'm wrong," she muttered. If Mercy's father *had* betrayed her family in some way, she wasn't sure she could bear it.

Dawn was chasing away the shadows by the time Elspeth got back to her cabin, and Grannie greeted her by name when she came inside. Elspeth was further relieved that Grannie didn't ask where she'd been. "Let me put on water for porridge," she said. "Then I'll tend the animals."

"I want you to go fetch your Aunt Mary," Grannie said. "We should be together while we wait for news."

"I'll go after breakfast. But I don't think she'll come."

"She must come!" Grannie snapped. "I'll fetch her myself if I have to—"

"No! No, I'll go." Elspeth didn't want Grannie walking the forest trails. Not now.

After milking the cow and choking down some breakfast, Elspeth dragged herself back outside. *Mo chreach,* she was weary. And heartsick. And frightened. Trying to stay alert, she hurried on to her aunt's cabin.

To her surprise, Aunt Mary wasn't alone. Maggie Gunn lay curled on the bed with her arms wrapped around her swollen belly. Her Hector had marched off with Grandda and the boys. "Maggie walked here last evening when she started having birth pains," Aunt Mary murmured to Elspeth. "She can't travel now. I need you to bring Morag here. She's birthed more babes than I have."

Elspeth trudged back home in a cold drizzle. With a sinking heart, she noticed a few pieces of laundry still hanging in the yard. Why hadn't Grannie brought it all in before the rain started? Was she having another bad spell?

Once inside, it was hard to tell. Grannie didn't call Elspeth "Peggy" or drift into the past, but she was furious that Elspeth had come back alone. "Maggie Gunn has got

another month to go before her time." Grannie stalked
across the room. "It's defiance, pure and simple."

Elspeth rubbed her forehead. Had she ever been so
tired? This made no sense, unless . . . could Grannie be
afraid to go out? It seemed unbelievable. Grannie could
stand up to anything!

Or maybe she couldn't. Not anymore.

"Grannie," Elspeth said, her voice trembling, "*please*
come with me. We can cut through the woods —"

"I will not leave this place!" Grannie grabbed Elspeth's
arm with surprising strength and shoved her toward the
door. "Go, and don't come back without them!"

Elspeth made sure Aunt Mary had plenty of hot water
and clean linens. She let Maggie, who was groaning horribly,
squeeze her hand as she labored to give birth to her child.
The baby came sometime near noon, a tiny, squalling girl.

Then Elspeth crawled up the ladder to her cousins' loft
and sank down on the bed. *It is too much to bear,* she thought
dully. She had promised Grandda to take care of Grannie,
and she had failed. Just as she had failed to learn who had
betrayed her family's trust. But finally her exhaustion
was stronger than her grief, her fear, her worry. Wrapped
in her mother's *arisaid* — the only comfort she had left —
Elspeth slept.

A musket blast woke her. Or was it Aunt Mary's scream? The two seemed to hang mingled in the air as Elspeth jerked from sleep. Although lengthening shadows told her the afternoon was growing late, she still felt groggy as she plunged down the ladder. But she snapped awake when she saw through the window perhaps a dozen men on horseback, milling in the yard.

Someone pounded on the door. "Open up!" a man yelled in harsh English.

Aunt Mary shrank against the far wall, a hand pressed over her mouth. Maggie's dark eyes were wide. Her infant let loose a thin wail.

The door shuddered with pounding. "I said open up!" the man yelled again. "Or, by God, we'll burn the place down around your ears!"

Elspeth felt frozen. It was happening, just as it had in Scotland.

The man yelled again, showering curses on the Scottish Loyalists. And Elspeth reached the bottom of her fear, and found a place of fierce anger. She strode to the door, jerked it open, and glared at the stranger. He was a man of middling size who looked more likely to be making shoes or growing barley than terrorizing women. He wore a dark tricorn hat planted on his head, and tucked through a slit in the brim was a sprig of pine.

"What be your business here?" Elspeth demanded.

The Patriot stared at her for a moment, startled.

Then a scowl hardened his features. He shoved her aside. She stumbled against the wall, and a bed warmer hanging there clattered to the floor. "This is the home of Robert MacKinnon and Duncan MacKinnon," he announced. "They are known to have risen against the provisional colonial government of North Carolina and are therefore outlaws."

"They're not here!"

"We'll see about that." The leader grasped the heavy trestle table and heaved it over. A stack of pewter plates and a crock crashed to the floor. Dried peas rattled across the room. Then half a dozen men shouldered into the cabin to continue the search.

Through it all, through the crashing and tearing and breaking, Aunt Mary crouched like a whipped dog. Maggie pulled herself slowly from the bed and sank into a corner, huddled protectively over her child. "We're three unarmed women, you filthy dogs! A pox on you all!" she spat in angry Gaelic. But Elspeth looked carefully at each man destroying her aunt's belongings, and then she stepped outside and surveyed the riders waiting in the yard. Tall Tam MacRacken was not there. She didn't recognize a man among them. But she would never forget their faces.

She walked back inside in time to see a man stuffing Aunt Mary's favorite candlestick into a sack. Another was gobbling a handful of dried cherries. "There's no sign of them," one Patriot reported, clattering down the ladder.

The leader looked at Elspeth. "Get them out." He jerked his head toward the two women.

Elspeth grabbed her aunt's arm. "Come along, Aunt Mary. Aunt Mary! You must come with me!" As she tugged her aunt toward the door, the Patriot reached into the hearth and pulled out a small log. One end was glowing red. He climbed halfway up the ladder and tossed the log into the loft.

The men left the cabin as Elspeth settled her aunt beneath a pine tree at the edge of the clearing. When she ran back inside, smoke was already filling the room. She heard the crackle of flames from the loft. "Maggie!"

"I'm here." Maggie crept from the smoke, moving painfully, coughing. Elspeth took the infant and towed Maggie outside to safety.

From across the clearing, Elspeth stared at the cabin. Smoke billowed from the open door and smashed window. Waves of heat shuddered across the clearing. A roaring crackle filled the afternoon.

"I didn't save a thing," Elspeth whispered, remembering the tales of her mother's quick thinking. Not a bowl, not a blanket. She put a palm against the rough orange bark of the pine tree to steady herself. She hadn't even saved her mother's *arisaid*.

She'd have to face that later. Right now she needed to get Aunt Mary, Maggie, and the baby to safety. Her own home was the closest—

Her own home. "Dear God," she whispered. Her skin prickled. Grannie was home alone. And those Patriots had been riding east.

CHAPTER II
THE DESIGN COMES CLEAR

It seemed to take a cold, lonely lifetime to get Aunt Mary, Maggie, and the baby to the MacKinnon homesite. Twilight was descending as they rounded the final bend. Elspeth held her breath, afraid to look. But the cabin appeared whole and sound through the trees— smoke still spiraling from the chimney, chickens still scratching in the yard. Mistress Blair's handwoven towel still waved on the clothesline like a cheerful greeting. Elspeth almost wept with relief.

Grannie met them at the door.

"Did the Patriots ride past?" Elspeth demanded breathlessly. "They burned down Aunt Mary's house."

Grannie shook her head. "I've seen no one. Inside now, quickly." She took charge with her old air of command, getting Maggie and the baby into bed.

Stiff with cold, Elspeth crouched gratefully by the hearth. She knew the Patriots could return at any time.

But she also knew that Maggie and Aunt Mary could go no farther that night.

Long after dark Elspeth crept back through the black forest and told Robbie what had happened. "And me here cowering like a rabbit," Robbie muttered angrily.

"And what help would you be in prison, Robbie Mac-Kinnon? None. Your place is right here for now. Do you hear? You will mind me on this!"

Her outburst surprised them both. A small animal rustled through the brush nearby.

"We'll see this through," Elspeth said. "Here, I brought you more food, and this old wool shirt of Grandda's, and a coverlet."

She sat still while he ate. The cold damp seeped through her skirt and petticoat, and an unseen brier scratched her cheek when she tried to get more comfortable. Even so, she suddenly was content to postpone hearing about the note she'd found at the Blairs'. Learning what it said might ease her mind. Then again, it might make her feel worse.

After Robbie had devoured his meal, he wrestled into the extra shirt. "Ah. That does help a bit. Now, about your note."

Elspeth's muscles tensed. "Could you make it out?"

"I could. I had plenty of time to study it." Robbie snorted without humor. "It said, 'Loyalist militia mustering Cross Creek 12th Feb.'"

Elspeth exhaled slowly. Bad—but not as bad as she'd

feared. The note might have spoken of the MacKinnons.

"The date of our muster was widely known, I believe," Robbie said. "Still, I think you'd better tell me where you found that."

So she told him the story—all of it. "I still don't know how Jennet's father fits in," she whispered finally. "But Mercy's father must have some part in it."

"Stay clear of both those men," Robbie ordered. "Do you hear? These are dangerous times, Elspeth. Don't get any more involved than you already are."

⋗

Robbie said only to stay clear of the **men**, Elspeth argued with herself as she hurried along the forested path to Cross Creek the next day. *He said naught about their families.* She wouldn't go into the village, where armed Patriots patrolled the streets. And she wouldn't stay to weave— she was needed at home. But she desperately longed to talk with Mistress Blair.

To her great relief, Elspeth found Mistress Blair alone at home. "Why, Elspeth!" She smiled as she rose from her loom, but her eyes were shadowed with concern. "Oh, child, you look exhausted. Come sit by the fire and tell me what's happening. We've been worried."

The sympathy in Mistress Blair's voice brought a lump to Elspeth's throat. Cornbread was baking in an iron

Dutch oven nestled into the coals. The room smelled of wet wool and walnut hulls—Mercy must have been dyeing yarn. Even now, knowing what she did, a big part of Elspeth wanted to stay forever.

"I needed to talk with ye," she said.

"Mint tea, first. There's water already hot."

Soon Elspeth sat across from Mercy's mother, drinking tea from a brown spongeware mug. She looked over the older woman's shoulder to the work area. The four-harness loom—*her* loom—hadn't been touched since she last worked it. The overshot pattern growing there was her own design. She'd measured warp threads of cream-colored wool and begun working the pattern in soft green. Her feet ached to feel the treadles. Her hands itched to take up the shuttles.

Mistress Blair sipped her tea. "Tell me what's happened."

"Ye ken that my grandda and two cousins marched off with the Loyalist militia and on to Moores Creek Bridge. I'm trying to care for my grannie and my aunt and a neighbor, too, who just yesterday brought a wee babe into the world."

"Merciful heaven." Mistress Blair put her mug down.

"The Patriots came to my aunt's place and burned it to the ground. They didna stop by Grannie's, but I'm thinking 'tis just a matter of time."

"Perhaps the men you speak of did all their mischief yesterday," Mistress Blair said slowly.

"I dinna know. The thing is ..." Elspeth hesitated, staring at her fingers. "Everything's come undone. And I've always felt ... felt safe here."

"You will always *be* safe here."

Elspeth shook her head. "Mistress Blair, I believe your husband is a Patriot. I need to know what that means for my family." There. She'd said it plain. She could face the truth. She had faced Duncan's death, and Grandda gone missing, and the Patriots. But she needed to know.

"Ah." Mistress Blair stared at the fire for a moment. "I have heard my husband say he loves you like a daughter. And that is as true today as it ever was."

"Aye?" She wanted so much to believe it.

"Elspeth, even when people hold ... strong beliefs, they can still care for people who believe differently. Do you understand?"

"Has Mr. Blair ever betrayed my family to the Patriots?" Elspeth's heart seemed to be beating very fast.

Mistress Blair held Elspeth's gaze. "No, he has not."

Elspeth blew out the breath she'd been holding. She still didn't know who had betrayed her family, or why. But the Blairs still loved her.

"Thank ye for speaking plain," she whispered. "It's been so hard. Neither my aunt nor my grannie is well. Grannie ... she wanders off in her mind. Sometimes she thinks I'm her daughter. Sometimes she gets angry and starts bletherin' over things that make no sense."

Mistress Blair shook her head. "When I think of what she's been through, what those soldiers did . . . well, it's understandable that her mind wanders. I pray she improves once this terrible trouble passes."

Trouble—it could be visiting Grannie right this moment. "I need to be away home," Elspeth said reluctantly.

Mistress Blair walked her to the door. "Elspeth, you will always be safe here. You do know that, don't you?"

Elspeth nodded. "Tell Mercy I'll be back when I can."

She turned into the lane, feeling better than she had in days. She could see this trouble through as long as she knew that her place with the Blairs, her weaving, waited at the end. For now, she needed to take care of her family.

And that meant finding out what bad blood lay between Grannie and Jennet's family. *If Mr. Blair hasn't betrayed us,* Elspeth thought, *it must have been Tall Tam.* She'd seen him watching her family—in church, in the woods, lately at the militia grounds. *Something* was behind his actions, and she intended to find out what.

Elspeth was tempted to march straight to the MacRackens' mill and demand answers. But she didn't dare, not without seeing to the ones at home first. Besides, she was cold. She missed her mother's *arisaid. But I can manage without it,* she told herself, and that knowledge was a comfort. Hugging her arms across her chest, she headed for home.

Only a few scattered houses lay between the Blairs' home and the forest that swallowed the land northwest of the village. As she passed one house, a shaggy brown dog ran barking to the road. "Wheesht!" Elspeth muttered. "I mean ye no harm." Then she noticed a familiar piece of fabric hanging on a line in the side yard: one of Mistress Blair's towels. *The lady here must be a friend of Mistress Blair's,* Elspeth thought, for the weaver had said she'd given pieces of cloth made from her Pine Bough design to her special friends—

Suddenly Elspeth's feet stopped moving. A faint, distant roaring echoed in her ears. She could hardly breathe. *It cannot be so,* she thought desperately. But at last the design of her problems came together in her mind, as if she had finally stepped on treadles in the proper order. She stood rigid as one thread slid into place in her mind, then another. Emboldened by her stillness, the dog nipped at her ankle, then trotted victoriously back to the sunny spot by the front door.

The clip-clop and creak of an approaching farm wagon finally brought Elspeth back to the moment. Clenching her jaw, she headed home.

When she reached her own clearing, the blue, white, and red Pine Bough towel still hung from the clothesline.

Elspeth grabbed it and marched into the cabin. Maggie sat by the hearth, nursing her babe. "*Elisaid!* You gave me a start," she scolded in a low tone. "Hush, now. Your poor aunt is resting."

"Where's Grannie?"

Maggie frowned. "Why, she just took the leavings out to feed the chickens—"

Elspeth stalked back outside and into the barn. Grannie stood in the dim aisle in front of the two stalls, tossing scraps from her apron to the half-dozen chickens pecking excitedly about her feet. Elspeth held out the towel.

Grannie tried to snatch it. "Give that to me! I must hang it back on the line!"

"Why?" Elspeth demanded in English. "What does this towel mean, Grannie?" When the old woman didn't respond, Elspeth stamped her foot. "Tell me! I know ye ken the question well enough!"

"*Elisaid,*" Grannie said hoarsely.

"Fine, then, I'll tell it. 'Tis a signal, if I dinna misguess. The Patriots here wear a sprig of pine in their hats or their buttonholes. And this is Mistress Blair's own design—the one she calls Pine Bough. I didna think twice when she cut her cloth into pieces to give to her friends. But I'm thinkin' now she gave the pieces only to Patriot friends."

Grannie's eyes were unreadable in the dim light.

"'Twas you that got word to the Patriots, wasn't it? Ye told where we'd be the night we took Mercy home. And ye told when the boys would be traveling the Wilmington Road." Elspeth's chest felt painfully tight and she sucked in a deep breath, the sharp tang of manure mingling with musty straw. "And ye insisted that I come home from the Blairs' the day that Patriot found me, though the weather was foul. Did ye tell him to watch for a wee girl wearing a cream-colored *arisaid* with plum stripes?"

Still Grannie didn't speak.

"Ye hung this towel on the line when the worst troubles started, and so it's been since. That's why ye tried so hard to get Aunt Mary here. And that's why the Patriots didna stop here when they rode by yesterday. Aye?" Elspeth swallowed hard. She felt a bit sick. "It was no' Mercy's father who betrayed us. 'Twas *you*—you and Mistress Blair. When I sat with her this day, she spoke of the hard times ye'd seen in Scotland. She spoke of what the soldiers did. I didna talk of that, Grannie. Never. How could she know your tales, if ye didna tell them?"

A man spoke from the doorway behind her. "I'd like to ken that myself." Elspeth whirled, barely managing to stifle her scream.

Then she flew into her grandfather's arms.

He grunted softly and eased her away. "Gentle there, lass."

Elspeth gasped in horror. Grandda's jacket was filthy and torn, the wool shirt beneath it stiff with dried blood. "You're hurt! Let me—"

"Nae, nae." He shook his head. "I found a good Scotswoman to bind it tight afore I headed for home. I'll mend."

"But ye shouldna be here!" Elspeth whispered. "Ye have to hide!"

"I know that well. It's slippery as an eel I've been these three days past."

"Robbie's safe hid, Grandda. He's—"

He put a finger over her mouth. "Thank God for that. But do not say where he is. 'Tis safer so." Then Grandda ran a hand over his hair, looking over Elspeth's shoulder at his wife. "I've been watching this place since just after dawn. I thought to wait 'til dark afore coming in. But I saw ye both go into the barn and not come out, and Elspeth lookin' sore aggrieved. I had to see what be what. And I heard enough, just now, to ken there's been trickery afoot. Will ye speak, woman, or do I need to shake it from ye?"

Grannie raised her chin defiantly. "'Tis true. What the lass said—'tis all true."

Hearing her grandmother speak English—slow and halting, but English—struck Elspeth as deeply as anything. "Ye've lied all this time!" she said, feeling light-headed. "Ye told me once that ye didna speak English. I remember it well!"

"I said I *didna* speak English," Grannie said harshly. "I never said I *couldna*."

Elspeth sank to the ground and leaned against the

wall. "You were so angry at Grandda when he enlisted. I thought you were afraid of being left alone again." She heard once more the sound of her mother's calico bottle shattering against the wall.

"But why?" Grandda demanded. "Good God, woman, why would ye work against the Loyalists?"

"It was clear to me soon enough that ye weren't inclined to take up arms with the Patriots. I knew *I* could no' turn your mind. Ye've never listened to me. So I saw no harm in helping the Patriots along a wee bit. I thought they might change your thinking where I could not."

Grandda glared. "It was no' just me the skunners tried to persuade! Elspeth was set upon, more than once! Did ye have no thought for the poor lass?"

"Elspeth is Peggy's own daughter," Grannie said, as if that explained everything.

"Morag." Grandda leaned against the wall and rubbed his forehead. He'd lost his cap, and his face was haggard. "What have ye done?"

"I did what I had to do." Grannie abruptly switched back to Gaelic, as if her rusty English couldn't keep up with her emotions. "I did what you would not! Have you forgotten how our family suffered at the hands of the British thirty years ago? If you have, I have not. You should have been eager to take up arms with the Patriots here—"

"I swore an oath of loyalty to the British king!" Grandda thundered.

"And I swore an oath to God, that I would fight the British with my dying breath!"

Moll stamped a hoof, a startling sound in the sudden silence. Elspeth stared at her grandparents, who stood face-to-face before her, breathing hard. *I have nothing left,* she thought numbly.

But something more needed to be aired. "I found a note at the Blairs', Grannie," she said. "It was to the Patriots and told when the Loyalist militia was to muster in Cross Creek. The note was smeared—as if written left-handed. Did you pack it into one of the baskets I carried to the Blairs?"

Grandda's fists clenched and twitched at his sides. "You sent such word to the Patriots? Your *grandsons* marched with that militia! God in heaven! Duncan was killed under the Loyalist banner!"

"*Donnchadh?*" Grannie took a step backward, as if struck; she hadn't known about Duncan's death. "I left off with everything after the boys ran off to enlist. I swear it, Angus." For the first time her voice trembled, and Elspeth remembered Grannie taking to her bed when Duncan and Robbie left home. "I didn't even know about the straw man left hanging for us to find." Grannie suddenly looked every bit of her sixty years, and more.

Go to her, Elspeth silently begged her grandfather.

But he could not. "You could have spoken to me of your feelings, Morag," he said heavily. "I would have listened."

"But you would not have understood."

"I suffered under British hands, too!" he flared. "And still—"

Grannie stabbed the air with her left forefinger. "There are things you do not know!"

Suddenly Grandda jerked erect. "Wheesht!" he hissed.

Elspeth had heard it, too—a quiet footfall outside the barn.

Grandda snatched at his stocking, but the knife was gone, no doubt lost in his flight from the field at Moores Creek Bridge. His broadsword was gone, too. He balled his fists, facing the door. Grannie silently picked up the grain scoop and jerked her head at Elspeth, signaling *Get behind us.*

Another footstep.

Sudden sweat dampened Elspeth's skin. She spied a sharp-bladed hoe leaning against the wall and slid toward it.

One more footstep. Grandda bent his knees, tensing for the spring. Elspeth wrapped her fingers around the stout hoe handle.

And then Tall Tam MacRacken stepped into the doorway, pistol in hand.

CHAPTER 12
OLD SECRETS REVEALED

Grandda leapt, the pistol fired, and Elspeth screamed, all at once. The shot flew wild. Grandda knocked Jennet's father flat on his back, then knelt over him, pinning MacRacken's hand to the ground. Grannie snatched the pistol. Elspeth raised her hoe, ready to strike.

"Speak, and speak quick," Grandda growled, "or I'll break your neck right here."

The younger man struggled ineffectually. "What the—why—I could have *killed* you, MacKinnon! What are you about?"

"That's what I'm asking you!"

"I meant no harm!"

"That's why you were sneaking about my place? With pistol cocked?" Grandda sat back on his heels. He took the pistol from Grannie, fumbled in MacRacken's *sporan* for powder and ball, and reloaded the gun. "Everyone, inside."

He pointed at the Pine Bough towel, now crumpled on the ground. "And hang that cursed thing back on the line."

Elspeth flung the towel over the line before following the others toward the cabin. Aunt Mary and Maggie met them at the door. "I heard a gunshot—why, *Angus*!" Maggie exclaimed, her eyes lighting with hope. "Thank God! Have you news of my Hector?" She dropped the iron fire poker she'd armed herself with.

"I'm sorry, Maggie, I do not." Grandda shoved Tall Tam into a chair. "You. Start talking."

Jennet's father looked angry. "You have this wrong, Angus. I was coming here to help."

"Then why were you creeping about?" Elspeth demanded.

"I was on my way to the cabin when I heard voices in the barn. Yours"—he pointed at Grannie—"sounded angry. Given what's been happening of late, I thought perhaps you were in trouble. So I pulled my pistol and started toward the barn. But when things went silent, I thought to approach with care."

Grandda scratched the stubble on his jaw with a thumbnail, eyes narrowed. Finally he nodded. "Fair enough. You can see how—"

"No, Grandda, wait! There's more he's not telling." Elspeth turned on Tall Tam. "You've been watching my family for weeks now. I saw you watching us in church, and at the muster field, and—"

"You caught my eye, no more," he interrupted. He didn't meet Elspeth's gaze, however. Instead he glanced toward Grannie, who sat staring at the floor.

"But you've come out here before," Elspeth insisted. "I *saw* you standing under yon tree, just watching this place!"

Tall Tam hesitated. "I came to speak to Morag," he said finally.

"And what business did you have with my wife?" Grandda's glare might have melted stone.

Grannie spoke into the stillness. "I'll tell you what business there is. It goes back thirty years, to The '45."

I knew it! Elspeth thought grimly.

"Wait!" Tall Tam interrupted. "Angus, I need to speak first of why I'm here now. Patriots coming to the mill sometimes speak free. I heard news this morning. When the Patriot militia won the field at Moores Creek, they didn't just capture men and guns. They got the muster rolls. They have the name of every man who marched against them."

"*Mo léir-chreach,*" Grandda muttered.

"I came to tell Morag. I thought she'd know who'd mustered with you—what families to warn." Tall Tam shook his head. "That towel you spoke of—I know that scheme, as do the local Patriots. But you've got Patriots from all over this colony hunting you now, man. That cloth won't save you from them."

Elspeth shivered. "You must go, Grandda! Go quickly!"

"Soon enough." Grandda looked at his wife. "But there's a tale that I think has needed telling for thirty years. I'll hear it before I leave."

Grannie stared at the flames flickering in the hearth. When she spoke, her voice sounded far away. "Young Jennet's grandmother once lived on Skye. Catherine and I were girls together, close friends. We married within a year of each other, started raising families. Then Prince Charlie landed in Scotland. Angus marched off to fight for him."

Elspeth leaned closer. "Did Jennet's grandda fight against the prince?"

"What? No, Ian Campbell did not, although many of his clan did. Ian tried to sit clear of it all. But when the British scoured the countryside, burning and killing, they took him by mistake. Ian was in prison for months, until he got someone to prove that he'd not marched with the prince."

Maggie's infant let loose a sudden wail from the bed, and Maggie went to tend her. Grannie didn't appear to notice the interruption. "While Ian was gone," she said, "Catherine's people turned her out. They thought he'd given word against them, you see. Ian tried to ride out the war and ended up with both sides thinking him the enemy.

"It was during that time that the British came to *my* door looking for Angus." Grannie's voice grew icy. "Twice they came, and I ended up hiding in the heather with my children, our home burned to ashes. Catherine found us. She begged me for food. I had a bit, thanks to Peggy. But I wouldn't share it with Catherine. I screamed at her and sent her away." Grannie's voice began to tremble. "And her with a hungry boy not two years old."

"You were protecting your own children," Aunt Mary said softly.

"It wasn't that." A tear ran down Grannie's scarred cheek. "The British left me so full of hatred that I even hated Catherine and Ian for not fighting against them. So I sent her off. And her boy died."

Grandda cleared his throat. "Two of our boys starved, too."

Grannie looked up at her husband. "There were children dying on all sides. Don't you see? All we Highlanders had left was our kinship. Our decency. And the British soldiers destroyed mine. They changed me into a woman who could turn her back on a friend. That I'll never forgive."

"Oh, Morag." Grandda stepped close and put a gentle hand on her shoulder. "Why did you never tell me all this?"

"Because you did not break!" Grannie wiped away another tear. "I've heard all the tales: How you took time to help a friend from the field at Culloden, even though it likely meant death for you. How you gave your shirt to a wounded man while you shivered in hiding. Even in prison, you shared your food."

It was shame that made Grannie bitter, Elspeth thought. *Not anger. Shame.* She wanted to wrap her arms around the old woman, but Grandda did so first.

Tall Tam rubbed his palms on his knees. "The story came down in my wife's family. Catherine never forgave Morag, and when Ian got out of prison, they moved away. I hadn't thought about the story in years, but when I came to Cross Creek and heard your names . . . it all came back."

"Yet Jennet wanted to be my friend," Elspeth murmured. How poorly she'd treated Jennet!

"I doubt that Jennet ever heard the tale. Catherine's been dead for years." Tall Tam shook his head. "But when I tried to introduce myself to your grandmother at the *céilidh,* I could tell that *she* still remembered and wanted no part of us. When I saw how lonely Jennet was, I came out here to try again. That was the day you saw me. Once I got here, I remembered the look on Morag's face and had second thoughts about opening old wounds. So I left."

Elspeth didn't know what to say.

"That day on the militia field, when I saw Angus and the boys march off, I decided that there was too much new trouble to let ourselves be haunted by events of thirty years past. But when you saw me, Elspeth, you got so angry—"

"Mr. MacRacken." Elspeth looked him square in the eye. "Please tell Jennet that I would be most pleased to visit her, as soon as I can."

He nodded and smiled. "That I'll do, child—"

A musket shot exploded outside. Elspeth looked out the window and felt her mouth go dry. Riders were pouring into the yard—a dozen or so men, heavily armed.

"No," Grannie moaned. "Not again. Not now."

Grandda crouched before her. "*Morag, mo chridhe,*" he said, "*feumaidh mi falbh.*"

Elspeth's eyes burned with unshed tears. *Morag, my heart, I have to leave.*

"We're here for Angus MacKinnon!" a man bellowed. "Send him out or we'll rip the house apart!"

Grandda calmly laid the pistol on the table. He pulled something from his pocket and pressed it into Elspeth's hand. Holding her gaze, he nodded once.

Then he strode to the door and flung it open. "No need for that," he announced. "I'm Angus MacKinnon."

After the Patriot soldiers took Grandda away, Elspeth opened her hand. His precious scrap of tartan cloth lay in her palm.

A NEW HOME

Mercy's mother looked startled when she opened the door. "Why ... Elspeth! Come in, child!"

Elspeth had avoided the Blairs' home for the past three months, and stepping inside now made her chest ache. The room still smelled of wool; the looms still called to her weaver's heart. She had once thought this place a safe haven, a true home. She knew better now, and she grieved.

"I wish to speak to ye," Elspeth began as soon as the door closed behind her. She knew they were alone because she'd waited unseen down the lane until Mercy walked her father toward town. "Ye betrayed my family to the Patriots! Ye betrayed my trust!"

Mistress Blair reached a hand toward Elspeth, then let it drop. "I was so sorry to hear about your cousin's death, and your grandfather's arrest. I never imagined—"

"Perhaps ye should have." Elspeth heard her voice

quivering and tried to firm it up. "I could have told ye that wars lead to terrible things."

The weaver took a deep breath. "Let me try to explain. As someone running a business and working to feed a family, I found the taxes imposed by the British government intolerable. Many people don't think the colonies are capable of controlling their own affairs. I know it *will* be difficult." She paused, collecting her thoughts. "I remember how difficult it was for me to take over the weaving business when my husband's sight failed—but now I glory in my newfound abilities! Because of what I've learned, I believe we American colonists *must* fight for our independence."

"But—but 'twas no' just about taxes and independence last winter." Elspeth folded her arms. "Those Patriots near frightened me to death! How could ye send me out to the forest to be set upon? And the first time we were stopped, Mercy was with us! How could ye do such?"

"It wasn't easy." Mistress Blair placed a hand on her belly, as if seeking comfort from her unborn child. "The Patriot men promised us that no one would be hurt. Your grannie just wanted to convince your grandfather to support the cause—"

"There was more to it than that!" Elspeth said sharply. "I found the note ye dropped, giving the date of the Loyalist muster."

"Ah." Understanding came to the weaver's face. "I did

wonder what became of that. Elspeth, that note made no difference. Everyone already knew about the muster."

The ache in Elspeth's heart eased just a bit.

"Before I started helping your grandmother, I hadn't done anything more than talk about independence." Mistress Blair sighed. "This seemed to be something I could contribute. And then I had the idea for using the towels as a signal—but I never dreamed how far things would go for your family. Neither did your grandmother, I'm quite sure of that."

Elspeth noticed a basket of quills, all expertly wound with fine brown wool, waiting for a weaver's eager hands to fit them into shuttles. She swallowed hard. "However did you and Grannie come to know each other?"

"Soon after you arrived in North Carolina, she stopped in with a friend from church who spoke a little English. Later she came back alone and asked about my weaving. She said she wished that every girl could learn a trade. I think she felt comfortable with me because we'd both been forced to take responsibility for feeding our children. And I think I gave your grandmother the chance to talk about the war in Scotland in a way she couldn't with other Scots. It's still too real and painful for Scottish people. I could simply listen."

Imagining Grannie and Mistress Blair having secret conversations was still hard. Postponing her next question, Elspeth wandered into the crowded work area. She touched the plain linen cloth on Mercy's two-harness loom, and lingered over a new coverlet growing on Mistress Blair's eight-harness loom. The four-harness loom, *her* loom, stood empty. A big part of Elspeth longed to slide onto the loom bench and get back to work.

"Did Grannie ask ye to teach me weaving just so she'd have a way to pass information?" she asked into the silence.

"No," Mistress Blair said firmly. "She wanted you to know how to earn a living. I needed help. And I loved having you. I thought of you as a second daughter. I still do. I'd welcome you back to the looms, Elspeth. I can't apologize for supporting the Patriot cause, but I won't let those beliefs get in the way of doing business with Loyalists—or of being friends with Loyalists."

Elspeth exhaled slowly. She'd long since forgiven Grannie her secrets. It seemed time to forgive Mistress Blair, too.

Then the door opened. "Mother, I—*Elspeth!*" Mercy flew to crush her friend in a hug before pulling her down on the bench. "It's been ever so long! I wanted to visit you, but Mother said I must wait until you came here. We heard about Duncan and your grandfather. We're so sorry. Have you been well?"

"We're getting by," Elspeth said stoutly. "But—I do have news. Robbie has joined the British army." After weeks of hiding, he had crept to the cabin one night to say his good-byes. He managed to evade capture as he made his way east to find the British soldiers.

"I'll keep him in my prayers," Mercy said soberly.

"I thank ye for that." Elspeth squeezed her friend's hand. "We also heard from my grandda last week. He thinks he's going to be released from prison soon. He and some of the other Loyalist prisoners have been talking, and..." Elspeth took a deep breath. "We're moving on. A big group of us, as soon as the men are released."

"Moving on," Mercy repeated, looking dismayed. "You're leaving North Carolina?"

"We're leaving the colonies. We're going to Canada. A place called Nova Scotia."

That news prompted a wail from Mercy, and her mother's face fell. Elspeth nodded. Grandda's news had come as a shock to her, too—but she'd come to understand. Her family needed to find a peaceful home, the home they'd crossed the Atlantic to find.

Mercy sniffed back tears. "I'll miss you terribly!"

"I brought something to remember me by." Elspeth pulled a small object wrapped in cloth from her pocket and placed it in Mercy's hand. Mercy pulled the cloth away carefully, revealing a piece of the shattered calico bottle. "That came from a bottle that saved my mother's and grannie's lives, back in Scotland. It...it got broken here last winter, but I think the glass is still pretty."

"Oh, it is," Mercy breathed, staring at the swirls in the shard. "I'll keep it safe."

"We have a gift for you, too," Mercy's mother said. She retrieved a folded coverlet from a wooden trunk and put it on Elspeth's lap.

"Oh!" Elspeth breathed. It was *her* coverlet—the one Mistress Blair had helped her design. She shook open the folds.

"Mother wove the panels off for you," Mercy told her. "And I sewed them together to make the coverlet. Father helped prepare the wool, so it's from all of us."

"What will you call the pattern?" Mistress Blair asked softly. "It's yours to name."

Elspeth considered, fingering the wool with a gentle hand. "I shall call it Thistle."

"Thistle?" Mercy looked perplexed.

"The thistle is a sign of Scotland," Elspeth explained. "When I sleep beneath this, it will remind me of home." For her real home, her *true* home, would always be Scotland.

Mistress Blair fetched some scraps of paper and presented them to Elspeth. "Here is your Thistle pattern draft, and several empty sheets." She fixed Elspeth with a firm gaze. "You must continue your work."

"Oh, I didna think . . . well, thank you." Elspeth stared at the draft, a string of tick marks on four lines indicating the treadling order. She'd never imagined weaving without Mistress Blair.

As Elspeth said her final farewells and headed out into the spring sunshine, she realized with both surprise and relief that she was glad to have these reminders of the Blair family to take to Canada. She didn't regret her time in North Carolina. She'd lost Duncan . . . but she'd gained some things, too.

Elspeth looked north for a moment, trying to imagine her new home. Nova Scotia—New Scotland. Grandda had said in his message that Nova Scotia was an island. Soon, she would again live by the sea.

Elspeth smiled, then began walking down the lane toward the trail that wound through the dark, dense pine forest to the cabin. She glanced thoughtfully at the blank bits of paper in her hand. Perhaps when she got back to the cabin she could mark down what she remembered of the last pattern she'd woven for Mistress Blair—Snowball, it was. With a wee bit of luck she might recall the Rosepath treadling, too. And in truth, despite not visiting the Blairs for three months, she'd had new pattern ideas, just waiting to be captured on paper. She need not go to Nova Scotia empty-handed.

Without realizing it, Elspeth quickened her pace. Her weaver's heart was light. She had work to do.

A Peek into the Past

LOOKING BACK: 1775

*A scene from the **Highlands**, the northern part of Scotland*

Thousands of Scottish families like Elspeth's sailed to America in the mid-1700s, escaping the desperate poverty and political turmoil in their homeland. During that time in Scotland's history, many Highlanders suffered tragedies just as terrible as those that Elspeth's family experienced.

Scottish immigrants settled in every American colony, but especially in North Carolina. About 15,000 Highlanders settled there—so many that the colonial government even issued a proclamation in both English and Gaelic!

Many Highlanders settled on good farmland along the Cape Fear River and prospered; some became leaders in the colony. Later immigrants, however, had to make their way inland from the river to find unclaimed land. Thousands settled in the towering long-leaf pine forests near the small town of Cross Creek.

Like Elspeth, these settlers found their new home strange. The English-

A cabin in the dense pine forests of North Carolina

speaking townspeople were foreign to them. Familiar crops like oats did not grow well in the sandy soil, and the forest felt dark and forbidding compared to Scotland's wide moors and green glens. A ballad written by one settler mourned, "In the gloom of the forest none of us will be left alive, with wolves and beasts howling in every lair."

Although many Scottish settlers felt homesick and out of place when they arrived in North Carolina, they did find some similarities with English colonists. Both English and Scottish women were expected to marry and manage their households. A woman rarely went into business unless she was single or widowed or, like Mistress Blair, her husband could not work. Very few girls learned a trade. Some did simple weaving at home, but the complicated overshot designs that Elspeth so loved were produced by professional weavers, who were nearly all men.

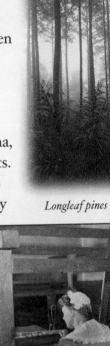

Longleaf pines

This is the draft of Gower Bark Penelope S. Boyd November The 9th 1846 by Aaron S. Boyd

Bed quilt Draft for Olly Whitley

Close-ups of overshot designs, and the pattern drafts used to produce them

As more and more Highlanders settled along the Cape Fear River, they began to feel at home in their new land. In their close-knit communities, they spoke Gaelic and played Scottish music, built Scottish churches, and sometimes wore traditional clothing, like Elspeth's *arisaid*. Although families worked very hard on their small farms, they soon had more food and better houses than they had ever had in Scotland. Some Scots made friends in Cross Creek. Most important of all, after enduring so much bloodshed and suffering in Scotland, the settlers hoped they had finally found a peaceful place to raise their families.

*A woman's **arisaid**, a length of wool belted at the waist and pinned at the neck to form a cloak*

But they were wrong.

By the time Elspeth's story opens in 1775, the first battle of the American Revolution had already been fought in Massachusetts. The war would soon spread throughout the colonies, and it would last eight long years.

The American Revolution was not just a war against Britain, however—it was also a civil war that turned neighbor against neighbor and tore families apart. Only about a third of American colonists were *Patriots,* who wanted independence from Britain. An equal number were *Loyalists,* siding with the British king, and the rest wanted to stay out of the conflict.

Loyalists and Patriots tried hard to win others to their cause. When persuasion failed, both sides used threats

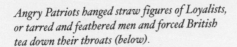

Angry Patriots hanged straw figures of Loyalists, or tarred and feathered men and forced British tea down their throats (below).

and violence, as the Patriots do in Elspeth's story. Some Patriots formed "Committees of Safety," which beat Loyalists or poured hot tar on them, burned their homes and barns, took their belongings, and slaughtered their animals. Loyalists sometimes committed equally vicious acts against Patriots.

In North Carolina, Patriots and Loyalists vied fiercely for the loyalty of the Scots, who were famed for their bravery in battle. The war was a horrifying prospect to many Scottish immigrants, however. Debates like the ones that took place in Elspeth's cabin must have been common as the worried Scots tried to decide whether to fight for or against the powerful British army. Some, particularly the earlier immigrants, joined the Patriots. Others tried to stay neutral. But in the end, many Scots, like Grandda, Robbie, and Duncan, chose to fight on the side of the British.

Many Highland Scots in the American Revolution dressed much like this Highland soldier of 1745.

These difficult decisions were faced by families of all backgrounds—and they were by no means left to the men alone. Like Mistress Blair and Grannie, many women in the colonies held strong opinions about the war and tried to influence events.

In North Carolina, more than 50 Patriot women in the town of Edenton signed a pledge to stop buying East India tea— a public protest that shocked people in England and America who believed women should stay out of politics. On the Loyalist side, Flora MacDonald, a heroine of the Highlanders' uprising in 1745, convinced many North Carolina Scots to support the king.

Flora MacDonald

About 1,500 Scots along the Cape Fear signed up to fight for the British. In February 1776, the men mustered in Cross Creek, as Grandda, Robbie, and Duncan do, and marched off to join British troops arriving by sea. On the way, they were ambushed by Patriots at Moores Creek Bridge. Dozens of Loyalists were killed, and more than 850 were captured and jailed, as Grandda was—some for more than four years.

Scottish Loyalists under fire at the Battle of Moores Creek Bridge

Few Cape Fear Scots ever fought for the British again, but for years after, Patriots burned and robbed their houses, arrested and hanged the men, and evicted families from their homes.

Loyalists in other colonies suffered similar treatment. Not surprisingly, huge numbers left America—about 100,000 in all. Thousands of Scots left North Carolina. Most, like Elspeth, migrated to Canada.

A Loyalist family leaving for Canada

Many Scots, however, considered themselves Americans and stayed to help shape the new nation. Almost half of the men who signed the Declaration of Independence were of Scottish descent, and the governors of nine of the original 13 states were, too. Today, 12 million Americans claim Scottish ancestry, and many aspects of Scottish culture are firmly woven into the fabric of American life.

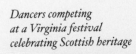

Dancers competing at a Virginia festival celebrating Scottish heritage

GLOSSARY OF GAELIC WORDS

NOTE: In Gaelic spelling, the letters "ch" stand for a sound similar to a very strong "h." (Think of the last sound in the name of the German composer, Bach.) In the pronunciations below, this sound is shown by the symbol ^ch.

arisaid *(AIR-a-sij)* — a length of woolen cloth worn around a woman's shoulders as a shawl or cloak

Beannachd leat *(BOWN-a^chk LOT)* — Good-bye

Beul sìos oirbh! *(bayl SHEE-us OR-uv)* — a Gaelic curse

céilidh *(KAY-lee)* — a social gathering, usually with music and sometimes with dancing and storytelling

Ciamar a tha thu? *(KIM-mur a ha oo)* — How are you?

Dé? *(jay)* — What?

Donnchadh *(DUN-uh-^chug)* — Duncan

Elisaid *(EL-uh-sij)* — Elspeth or Elizabeth

feumaidh mi falbh *(FAY-mee mee FALL-uv)* — I must leave

Gabh mo lethsgeul *(GAHV mo LESH-gul)* — Pardon me

Mo chreach! *(mo ^cHRE^cH)* — an exclamation of surprise and apprehension, similar to "Good heavens!"

mo chridhe *(mo ^cHREE-ya)* — a term of affection that means "my heart"; my darling

Mo léir-chreach! *(mo LAYR-^chre^ch)* — a strong exclamation of astonishment and fear

sporan *(SPOR-an)* — a carrying pouch worn at a man's waist

Glossary of Scots-English Words

afore—before
bannock *(BAN-nuck)*—a small oatcake fried on a griddle
blether *(BLEH-ther)*—talk nonsense
bonnet—a man's soft, flat cap
cack-handed—left-handed
canna—cannot
crowdie—a dish made from oatmeal and cream
da—father
didna—did not
dinna—do not
doesna—does not
grandda—grandfather, grandpa
ken—know
lad, laddie—a boy or young man
lass, lassie—a girl or young woman
nae—no or not
no'—not
numpty gowks—stupid fools
plaid—a long piece of tartan cloth worn over one shoulder
sea tangle—a variety of edible seaweed
skunner—a disgusting person
stramash *(strah-MAHSH)*—a commotion or argument
tartan—a distinctive pattern of colored lines and bands
    that cross at right angles; a cloth woven in this pattern
Wheesht!—Be quiet!
wi'—with
wouldna—would not

AUTHOR'S NOTE

In 1783, the village of Cross Creek merged with Campbellton, another settlement just a mile away. The new town was named Fayetteville after a Patriot hero of the Revolutionary War. Today Fayetteville is a busy city, and it is difficult to find traces of the town Elspeth would have known. Much of the landscape where Elspeth roamed, including the site of her church, is now part of a large military base called Fort Bragg. The longleaf pine savanna ecosystem that dominated that landscape has almost disappeared as well. An exhibit at the North Carolina Museum of Natural Sciences in Raleigh provides a glimpse of what the area once looked like, and a few artifacts from early Scottish settlers are on display at the Museum of the Cape Fear in Fayetteville. The site of the fateful battle of 1776 has been preserved, fortunately, and a visit to Moores Creek National Battlefield makes it easy to imagine what happened to the Highlanders who fought there.

Since so few remnants of this time and place remain, I am particularly indebted to a number of historians who provided assistance. Timothy Boyd, Education Technician at Moores Creek National Battlefield; Bruce J. Daws, Historic Properties Manager of Fayetteville; and Dr. Michael Newton, University of Richmond, shared their time and knowledge. Beverly A. Boyko, former Archaeological Collections Manager at Fort Bragg, provided a very special tour of Fort Bragg and the Longstreet Church site. I'm especially grateful to William S. Caudill, Director of the Scottish Heritage Center at St. Andrews Presbyterian College, for his ongoing help.

Finally, heartfelt thanks go to my patient family for their perpetual encouragement; to my wonderful writing circle for their always-helpful feedback; and to my friends at Pleasant Company, who put as much love and care into each book as I do.

ABOUT THE AUTHOR

Kathleen Ernst is a writer and historian who learned to weave on an antique loom while working at a large historic site. She enjoys researching historical novels as much as writing them. From warping a loom to baking corncakes over an open fire, she likes to try the tasks her characters undertake whenever possible.

Ms. Ernst's first book in the History Mysteries series, *Trouble at Fort La Pointe*, was nominated for the 2001 Edgar Allan Poe Award for Best Children's Mystery; her second, *Whistler in the Dark*, was nominated for the 2003 Agatha Award for Best Children's/Young Adult Mystery.

She has also written four novels set during the Civil War: *Ghosts of Vicksburg, Retreat from Gettysburg, The Bravest Girl in Sharpsburg*, and *The Night Riders of Harpers Ferry*. When she's not busy writing books, she helps develop and script instructional television programs.